INTENTIONS 2

D1525419

BY

NONA DAY

SOUL PUBLICATIONS

Same Night

Cache

My left arm and ankle were throbbing with pain. During my tumble down the stairs my phone had fallen out of my hand; although it was painful, I scooted closer to my phone and tried calling Noble's phone. I screamed out in frustration when I remembered that I had fallen down the stairs because I was rushing to the front door to tell him that he left his phone. Dinah called saying she was having contractions, and he left in a hurry so he could meet her at the hospital.

Panic started to set in. Calling 911 would take forever, so I quickly dialed Amoy's phone number praying she answered, and on the second ring she did. I couldn't hold my composure as I told her to hurry over. She didn't ask any questions but assured me she was on the way. I started scooting to the downstairs bathroom and sharp pains shot through my lower abdomen. Tears flowed down my face as I looked down at the blood between my thighs.

After making it to the bathroom, I carefully pulled myself up to sit on the toilet. With my good arm, I removed my jeans and panties. Using a wet washcloth, I wiped the blood from between my legs as I prayed to God to save my baby. I needed Noble there with me, but I had no way of contacting him. After wiping myself clean, I realized I wasn't bleeding anymore. The problem was, I didn't know if that was a good or bad thing, because I didn't know if I had miscarried our baby or not. It didn't take long before I heard Amoy calling my name. Noble must've left the door unlocked as he dashed out of the house. She rushed in the bathrooms I was still sitting on the toilet.

"What happened? Where's Noble?" she asked nervously.

"I fell down the stairs, and he went to the hospital. I think Dinah's in labor. I need to get to the ER. I've been bleeding, and my ankle and arm is in a lot of pain," I explained. Amoy looked in the sink at the blood-soaked washcloth. I could see the worry in her eyes.

"I'll grab you something to put on," she said charging out of the bathroom.

"I have some clothes in the top right drawer of the dresser," I yelled out to her.

She came back with a pair of tights. After struggling to help me put them on, she helped me stand up.

"Put your weight on me," she said.

I threw my right arm over her shoulder and she wrapped her left arm around my waist. After helping me get in the car, she called the ER to let them know we were on the way.

*****

When we arrived, they took me to the exam room. Amoy sat with me until it was time for the nurse to examine me. She asked me a thousand questions. As they cared for my dislocated shoulder and sprained ankle, the only thing I wanted to know was if my baby was still alive. Dr. Anthony, my gynecologist, finally arrived. I laid back with my feet in the stirrups, holding my breath as she examined me.

"Is my baby okay?" I asked anxiously after she was done.

"There's a small tear in your uterus. That's what caused the bleeding. We're going to do an ultrasound to hear the heartbeat and check the baby's movement," she said, smiling at me.

She tried to look confident and positive, but I knew a tear in the uterus could cause a miscarriage. My heart was pounding. Amoy had called Dachon, so he could get in touch with Noble. I prayed he would get here soon, because I didn't know how I would handle it if I lost our baby. The irony it would be if he gained a child and I lost ours at the same time. Anger started to set in my heart. If he hadn't been rushing to get to Dinah, I wouldn't be here losing our child. Just as Dr. Anthony was spreading the jelly over my belly, Noble barged into the room. His face was covered with regret and concern.

"I'm sorry, Dr. Anthony, I told him he couldn't come in here," the short, white nurse explained. Dr. Anthony looked at me for assurance that Noble's presence was okay. I nodded my head.

"It's okay. He can stay," Dr. Anthony told the nurse.

"What happened?" Noble asked walking over to me.

"You left your phone, so I tried catching you before you left. But I fell down the stairs," I said.

He closed his eyes for a brief moment. "I'm sorry."

"Okay, let's hear that heartbeat," Dr. Anthony said. She started sliding the instrument over my belly. The room was completely silent as I held my breath waiting to hear my baby's heartbeat. I squeezed Noble's hand from fear of the silence in the room. Noble stood by my bedside as rigid as a block of cement. Our eyes, along with Dr. Anthony's, were glued to the monitor. I glanced at Dr. Anthony and the concern on her face caused tears to slide down the side of my face.

"My baby," I cried softly. All that could be heard through the room was my soft cries as they turned into loud sobs. Noble tried consoling me, but I didn't want him to touch me.

"Get off me!" I screamed as I tried sitting up.

"Don't move," Dr. Anthony demanded softly, pointing at the screen. She slid the instrument farther down my belly. My heart started to pound along with the rapid little heartbeat. Dr. Anthony looked at me and smiled. I cried and laughed, overjoyed with hearing my baby's heartbeat.

"Is the baby okay?" Noble asked.

"The heartbeat is strong, and it's moving. I'm going to run some tests to make sure everything else is okay, so you'll be here with us for at least a day," Dr. Anthony said.

"Thank you," I said graciously.

"You're welcome. I'll give you two some time alone. I'm going to schedule a few tests," she said before leaving the room. Noble pulled a chair up beside the bed and sat down.

"Damn baby, I'm sorry I wasn't there," he said remorsefully.

"Did Dinah have the baby?" I asked.

"She was getting ready to go into the delivery room when Dak showed up," he said.

"Is she here at Emory?" I asked.

"Yea; on another floor," he replied.

"Go see your baby. We're okay," I said touching my belly. I could tell by the look in his eyes that he was conflicted on whether to stay or go.

"I'm not mad at you. I just had a moment," I assured him. I wasn't going to let my emotions cause him to miss the birth of his child. That brief moment of possibly losing my baby was scary and painful, but I wanted him to enjoy seeing the birth of his first baby.

A Few Days Later

Dachon

It had been a few days since I found Ma's letter, and I knew this would be too much for Amoy to handle. She had finally moved past my father being the cause of her parents' death. It would break her and us if she knew that he intentionally killed them. There were so many questions I needed answered regarding my father's actions. *Who blackmailed him to kill her parents? Why did they want her parents dead?* Those were the most important questions.

I had been avoiding Amoy, because I knew I held a secret that she needed to know, but I needed answers before I revealed what I knew. To find the answers, I needed to take a trip home; but first, I needed to fill Jar in on what I found out. I didn't want to take the chance of Aunt Belle finding out what truly happened before I could tell him. We were at Noble's lounge having a drink. The place wasn't due to open for a few hours, so it was just Noble, Jar, a few workers, and me. Jar and I sat at the bar while Noble stood behind the bar making sure it was stocked.

"Congratulations," Jar said as we raised our glasses to the birth of Noble's baby girl. We chugged down our shots of Hennessy Ellipse. After we toasted to Noble's baby girl, we took another shot to friendship and family.

"Thanks," Noble said solemnly.

"Damn, you don't sound like a proud father. I mean I know it ain't the circumstances you wanted to bring yo first born into the world, but that's yo lil seed, nigga," I said.

"I know, but something doesn't feel right. I know in my gut it ain't my child, and I don't wanna create a bond until I know for sure," I explained.

"Nigga, you just scared Cache gon' trip about you spending time with yo seed," Jar added.

"She's actually being understanding. I still feel like shit for leaving her when she almost lost our baby," Noble confessed.

"Man, that wasn't yo fault. Shit happens," Jar said shrugging his shoulders.

Noble and Jar strategized about taking over a few spots from his Aunt Belle. It all seemed crazy how they were feuding with each other when they could just work together. Aunt Belle wasn't willing to let Jar run the operation by her side. She was treating him like he wasn't family, but if it wasn't for Jar's father, Aunt Belle wouldn't have shit to run. I prepared myself to drop the bombshell on Jar as they talked.

"I'm taking a trip home. I need you to ride with me," I said looking at Jar.

"We gotta kill somebody or something?" Jar asked seriously.

I chuckled. "I can kill by myself. This is an informative trip that I need you to be a part of."

"What's up?" Noble asked. I pulled the letter from my back pocket and placed it on the table. Jar picked the letter up and started reading it. Noble looked at me with concern. After Jar was done reading the letter, he placed it on the table and Noble started reading.

"What time we leaving?" Jar asked through gritted teeth.

"First thing in the morning. I know a few old ones I can ask about my ol' man's dealings," I told him.

"Damn, this shit crazy," Noble said giving me back the letter.

"I'll be at your place first thing in the morning," Jar said, standing up. He didn't wait for me to acknowledge his statement before walking away.

"Somebody is about to die tonight," Noble said, watching him walk out of the lounge.

I just shook my head, because I knew finding out my father intentionally killed his parents enraged him. I made a quick call to Nova to see if she could keep him company tonight. Their strange, platonic relationship worked for them, and their chemistry couldn't be denied by everyone around them. Just like me, I was sure he was eager to find out who was responsible for their deaths. I was angry with my father, but I understood why he did what he did. It was either kill strangers or Ma and I would die because of his gambling habit. The reason I was living now was because Amoy and Jar's parents were dead.

After leaving Noble's lounge, I had to stop by my club to make sure everything was setup before it opened. Lisa had gained a permanent position as head manager. My previous manager, Chantel called and informed me that she wouldn't be returning. Her sister was in a bad house fire and suffered third degree burns. She was staying to help her through recovery and to assist with her four-year old niece.

Luckily, the child was with her father when the fire occurred.

*****

When I arrived at the club, Lisa was giving orders like she had been in charge since day one. I didn't interfere with her, because she was doing a good job. The only time I stepped in was when there was a complaint from one of the workers. So far, things had been running smoothly. A few dancers were dancing on the poles to Wale's Pole Dancer. Eva was recording footage to post on the social media sites.

"Let's get you in a few pictures," Eva said. I wasn't fond of taking pictures, but I'd do what I had to in order to promote my club. I sat in a chair in the middle of the dance floor, and the dancers posed with me in a few sexy pictures. Hot Girl Summer started playing and all the girls started twerking. Voluptuous, round asses were all around me. Lisa came over and straddled my lap. She wound her hips and massaged my chest and arms.

"Don't stop. This is great footage," Eva said. When I felt my dick growing, I knew it had gone too far.

"I knew you still felt something," she said smiling at me. Her pussy was rubbing against my bulge.

"My dick feels it, but I don't," I said. I tapped her on the ass and moved her away.

I made my way to my office and flopped down on my sofa. I hadn't slept much since finding Ma's letter, so I fired up a blunt and took a few hits. It didn't take long before I was drifting off to sleep. I was awakened by an angry Amoy.

"Now I know why you've been avoiding me. You still fucking her!" She screamed angrily.

"What? What da fuck you talking about?" I asked still trying to wake up.

"I saw the video of her giving you a lap dance. Nigga, yo dick was hard as fuck when you stood up," she stated. I didn't know Eva was going to post that footage, because all footage had to be cleared by me beforehand.

"It's just a fuckin' video, Amoy. Ain't shit going on between me and Lisa," I said, standing up.

"Whatever nigga. I knew I couldn't trust yo ass," she said, staring up at me.

I chuckled. "You never trusted me. Agreeing to let Lisa work with me was a part of your plan. You wanted me to fuck up, so you'd have your excuse to end this shit. Well, let me help you with that. Get da fuck out."

"What?" she asked incredulously.

"You heard me. Get da fuck out. You have the excuse you've been looking for," I said, flopping back down on the couch. She stood watching me as I fired up the blunt again.

"So you admit you're still fucking her?" she asked hurtfully.

"I ain't admitting shit. I'm just giving you what you want," I said, staring up at her.

She stood silently as I inhaled the blunt. I could tell she wanted to say more, but she had too much pride. As I watched her walk out of my office, I wanted to go after her, but I needed this break from her. Ma's letter made me feel like I was betraying Amoy. She deserved to know the truth about her parents' death. I just needed time to gather information before I told her what truly happened to them.

I decided to pour myself into work to get the letter off my mind, but before I could, Lisa strolled into my opened office door with a smirk on her face. Amoy had every reason to be suspicious of Lisa. On numerous occasions she had made it obvious to me that she was still interested in me, but my feelings weren't the same. She sat down in the chair in front of my desk and crossed her legs.

"I saw Amoy leaving. She looked upset. Is everything okay?" she asked.

"Your only concern is the club; Amoy is my concern," I told her. She stood up and walked to the door before turning to face me.

"If she wasn't in the picture, would I stand a chance?" she asked.

"I can't answer that because she's in my life. Is there another reason you came to my office?" I asked.

"Yea; I need to find a place to stay. I'm tired of living out of the hotel," she said.

"I'll see what Noble has that's affordable for you. I don't feel right charging you for one of my places, and it wouldn't look right for me to let you live rent free. Hope you understand," I said.

"Fine," she said. She waited a moment. "Also, Eva wanted me to inform you that a professional photographer is coming to take pictures of you and the staff tomorrow."

"Tell her to reschedule it. I'm going out of town for a couple of days," I informed her.

"Where are you going?" she asked. I replied with a stare. My movements were no concern of hers. She walked out the office making me wonder if her working for me was a good idea.

Noble

I sat beside Dinah's bed holding the baby as she slept peacefully. She was a healthy, beautiful baby at six pounds and five ounces with a head full of jet-black hair. We hadn't named her yet. I started thinking of names but couldn't come up with any. A part of me wanted to love this beautiful child with all my heart, but something deep inside me felt off. I studied the baby's face trying to find some kind of resemblance of me but couldn't see any. She didn't have my family's trademark which was our wide nostrils. The one thing I didn't want to do was not claim her before I knew for sure she wasn't mine. As soon as Dinah woke up, I needed her to agree to a blood test.

"Isn't she perfect," Dinah said finally waking up.

"Yea, she is. What are you going to name her?" I asked; my eyes were still glued to the baby. I felt guilty about not being able to say the baby was mine.

"I don't know. I thought you could help me name her," Dinah said, shrugging her shoulders.

"I think we should get a blood test before I'm a part of that decision. Don't you think that would be best?" I asked.

An aggravated look immediately settled on Dinah's face. I didn't want to upset her, but I needed to know for sure this baby was mine before I built a bond with her. Before she could respond, the room door came flying open. Penelope, Dinah's mom, came barging into the room. I was surprised to see her there. She never gave a damn about Dinah or any of her other kids.

"Let me hold my grandbaby," she said, walking over and standing directly in front of me. She took the baby out of my arms and started kissing and playing with her. "Did he sign the birth certificate?" she asked, looking at Dinah.

"I'm right here; you can ask me," I said, looking up at her.

"Well, did you?" she asked, giving the baby to Dinah.

"No, I didn't," Dinah said.

"And why the fuck not? This child looks just like you," she asked angrily.

I wasn't going to entertain her, so I stood up and walked out of the room. Penelope and I had never gotten along. She thought I was a cash machine when I was dating Dinah; she was always begging Dinah to get money from me. I was sure she hoped the baby was mine thinking it would be beneficial to her some kind of way. The only time she was ever nice to Dinah was when she had her hand out.

I was waiting by the elevator to go to Cache's room when Penelope approached me. She stood in front of me with her long, black wavy hair. Her breasts were too big for the low-cut blouse and her jeans were too tight. She looked younger than forty and acted like a ratchet ass adolescent most of the time.

"You will take care of Dinah and your child," she said sternly with her hand on her hip.

"Yes, I'll take care of my child. I'm going to give Dinah a couple of days to recuperate; then we'll have a blood test. If the baby is mine, I'll be there for her and Dinah. But I will not put a damn dime in your hand. I know that's your concern."

"My concern is making sure my daughter and grandchild is provided for by the father of the child, and that *is* you," she said before walking away. I shook my head as I entered the elevator regretting getting involved when Dinah after I did my bid.

Cache was laughing and talking with a nurse when I walked into the room. She informed me that all the tests came back negative, so she was being released. Her main concern was missing her classes, because she was going to have to stay off her feet for a couple of weeks because of the tear in her uterus and sprained ankle. My concern was getting her back to my house and making sure she got the proper amount of rest.

*****

Neither of us spoke on the ride to her house. She wanted to stop by and pick up a few things from her place. I was sure she had questions about Dinah's baby, because the baby was deep on my mind also. I couldn't shake not feeling like a new father. This was a time I was supposed to be beaming with pride, but there was too much doubt clouding my mind. Getting the paternity test as soon as possible was a must.

When we arrived at Cache's house, her father was walking out of her apartment. His facial expression was a mixture of fear and worry as he rushed to the passenger's side of the car.

"What happened? Are you okay?" he asked worriedly.

"I'm fine, Daddy. Just a sprained ankle. I dislocated my shoulder but it's all good now," she said as he helped her out of the car.

"Come on. I'll carry you inside," he said.

"That's my job. I'll get her," I said.

He ignored my response and scooped her up in his arms. I got out and walked to the passenger's side of the car.

"You've done enough," he said, walking past me.

I chuckled and followed him to the door. I wasn't surprised that he was upset about what happened to Cache. Fathers were always over-protective of their girls. I opened the door to let him in and he sat Cache in the den on her chaise. He turned to face me.

"You get my daughter pregnant and let her fall down the stairs?" he asked.

"Daddy, how do you know I'm pregnant and that I fell?" Cache asked.

"I saw your talking ass cousin Stephanie at Walmart last night. I want to know how come I didn't know I was going to be a grandfather," he said. His question was directed more toward me than Cache.

"Cache wasn't ready to tell you. I supported whatever decision she made regarding the pregnancy," I told him. He gave Cache his attention.

"Sorry Daddy. I just wasn't ready to tell you. I know you always told me to finish school before starting a family," she said.

He turned back to face me. "You gon' take care of my daughter and…"

"You don't have to give me empty threats. I'll always be here for her and our child," I assured him.

"My damn threats aren't empty. Don't let the age fuck you up into thinking I'm light-weight," he said.

"Daddy, stop being dramatic," Cache said.

He walked over and stood over Cache. "My baby girl having a baby."

She smiled up at him. He sat down on side of the chaise and gave her a tight hug. When my phone rang, I left them in the den to talk.

"Yeah," I said, walking into the living room.

"When you gon' come sign the birth certificate?" Dinah asked.

"I'll sign it when the paternity test comes back. You won't be running to Maury's backstage sofa on me in the future. Let's get it over with, so we can know for sure," I told her.

"We need a ride home tomorrow." She ignored my request for a paternity test.

"I'll be there to take you home," I told her. I wasn't going to neglect her, because of the baby. I'd be there until I knew for sure. If she insisted on not giving me a paternity test, I'd do one of those home tests.

"Good." She ended the call. I went back into the den.

"I don't know why you got out of the car. You staying with me," I told her.

"I was wondering the same damn thing. That's how you step up and be a man. I'm gon' get out of y'all's way. Call me if she doesn't want to rest that ankle. She can be hard-headed," he said nodding his head at me. I chuckled and shook his hand after he held it out for me.

After her father left, I retrieved the things she wanted to take to my place. Most of the items were her books for school. I hoped she planned to ask her professors to send her assignments home because she wasn't going to class. When I came back into the den, she was scrolling through her phone.

"She's beautiful," she said, staring at the phone.

"Who?" I asked.

She looked up at me with sad eyes. "Your daughter. What's her name?"

"We haven't named her yet. I want to take the test before I sign the birth certificate," I informed her.

"If it is, I know you will be a great dad to both our kids. If it's not, you'll be a great dad to this child. I won't make this more stressful for you," she said.

"You said *our kids*." I smiled at her.

"Yes, I know I won't be the child's biological mother. But that's a part of you. I will be a mother to Dinah' child like she's my own flesh and blood without overstepping my boundaries," she explained. I wasn't worried about Cache. Dinah was going to be the problem.

"I know this is more stressful for you than me. I love you for sticking this out with me," I said to her. She kissed me softly on the lips.

Amoy

Dachon had left town without informing me. I called and texted him numerous times, but I still hadn't gotten a reply. The only way I knew he was out of town was because Cache heard him tell Noble he would be back in a couple of days. I guess he was truly done with me. Seeing them on that video made me feel insecure. They had history, and it was obvious he cared about her. I didn't know if what we have was strong enough to keep him faithful. Lisa didn't hide the fact that she wanted Dachon, so maybe, subconsciously, agreeing to let Lisa work for him was a test. I was only asking for trouble by allowing them to work together, but I didn't want to show my insecurities by complaining about it.

On top of that, Jarvis was out of town, as always, leaving me here to deal with Aunt Belle. Her complaints of me being with Dachon were getting tiresome and today was no different. She was in my kitchen cooking and rambling nonstop about Jarvis going against her. I sat quietly scrolling through my phone.

"I'm telling you, Amoy, that boy don't mean you no good. His father wasn't shit, and he ain't gon' be shit," she said.

"Aunt Belle!" I yelped loudly. She looked at me with wide eyes.

"Please stop it. He's not responsible for what his father did. I would truly appreciate it if you would stop demonizing him. I love him, and you have to accept that," I said softly. It was the first time that I actually admitted to loving him.

She shook her head. "Watch my words. That boy is going to break your poor, little naïve heart." I prayed Dachon didn't prove her right.

I was relieved to hear my doorbell ring, so I hurried out of the kitchen. Nova was coming over to have dinner with us. She had developed a huge crush on Jarvis, but I didn't think he had noticed it. He thought she was weird, because he was used to ratchet girls. Nova was a totally different breed of woman. As per usual, Nova stood on the other side of the door in her multi-colored, uncoordinated clothes. We went to the den and I popped the bottle of wine she had brought with her while Nova made herself comfortable on the sofa.

"You feeding homeless people now?" Aunt Belle asked walking into the den. She was looking at Nova like she was disgusted.

"No Aunt Belle, and that's rude. This is my co-worker Nova Lee, but we call her Nova," I said smiling at Nova. Her wooly, wild mane was untamed on her head. She had the smoothest milk chocolate complex that I'd ever seen. Even in the dim den it was like the sun was shining on her and making her skin glisten.

"Can I use your bathroom?" Nova asked, shooting up from her seat.

"Yea; down that hall and second door to the right," I said. Nervously, Nova hurried out of the room. Aunt Belle shook her head when Nova zoomed past her.

"Watch your jewelry around her. She might steal it, and what's with her clothes?" Aunt Belle asked.

I giggled. "She's eccentric."

"She's damn crazy for coming out the house looking like that. I'm done cooking, so I'm gone. I love ya and I'll call you tomorrow. Tell Jar we need to talk whenever he gets back," she said. She gave me a hug and a kiss on the cheek. Whether she agreed with me dating

Dachon or not, I was always going to love my aunt. I just needed her to respect my choice to be with him. She didn't have to like him, but she had to stop disrespecting him.

About ten minutes later, Nova came back into the den. I was lounged on the sofa gulping down the delicious wine she brought with her.

"Girl, where did you get this wine? I've only had one glass and I can feel it. And the shit taste good as hell," I said, refilling my glass.

"Where's your aunt?" she asked, looking around.

"She's gone. Thank God," I said.

"Sorry, but she gives me the creeps," she said, pouring a glass and firing up a blunt. I was shocked because I didn't know she smoked.

I giggled. "No apology needed. She creeps me out sometimes."

She smiled. "Oh and I made the wine at my parents' farm."

I laughed. "Your parents' own a farm in Atlanta?"

"They live in Alpharetta. I make the wine out of the grape orchid along with other things," she said.

"Girl, you need to bottle this shit up and sell it," I told her. She laughed, but I was serious.

"It's just for my personal consumption," she said smiling. "Now, tell me what you did to try and ruin your relationship."

My eyes grew wide. "What makes up think I tried to ruin it?"

"Because you are scared of letting him get too close, so the best thing to do is push him away," she said. I told her what happened, and she laughed.

"Amoy, you wanted that man to do some foul shit so bad, you overreacted on the smallest thing," she said.

"I just want to know I can trust him. What's wrong with that?" I asked.

"So you put him to a test to break the trust that you don't have in him? That doesn't make sense, Amoy."

"Well, what do you suggest?" I asked.

"I suggest you stop the battle between your heart and mind. Choose one and follow it," she said.

"If I choose my mind, I'll have to let him go. But I love him, and I don't want to let him go," I told her.

"Well, let your heart lead." She took another hit from the blunt. She passed it to me, and I inhaled deeply. I felt like I was going to cough up a lung.

"Damn you grow this shit too?" I asked still coughing. She laughed and nodded her head.

It took no time for the weed to have me giggling for no reason. The wine and weed had me horny as fuck. I grabbed my phone.

"I'll be right back," I told Nova.

I went into my study and pulled off my jeans and panties. While lying on the couch, I played in my pussy until it was dripping wet. My phone was propped perfectly to record everything. After I creamed all over my fingers, I sent the video to Dachon's phone. I went to the bathroom and cleaned up before joining Nova back in the den. Nova was a true stone head, because she was on her second blunt. I had only hit the first blunt a couple of times. Maybe I was too high to tell, but she didn't even seem high. I smiled when my phone alerted me of a text message. I knew it was Dachon.

I'm gon' fuck da shit outta you when I get back

I smiled and poured myself more wine. Nova may not sell this wine, but she was going to sell some to me. I enjoyed having Nova at my house. She brought a sense of happiness and peace. I wished Cache could've been here with us, but Noble wasn't letting her out of the house. The only way he agreed to let her attend her classes was if she went in a wheelchair. She raised all kinds of hell about it before she agreed. He was going to pay one of his workers to get her from class to class and back home. Noble was the perfect match for Cache, because he didn't let her get her way when she threw tantrums.

Valdosta, Ga

Dachon

"What da fuck you smiling at yo phone for?" Jar asked as we sat at the bar in the club Noble owned.

I smiled at him. "Yo sister a freak."

"Man, gone with that bullshit," Jar said with a scowl on his face. I laughed.

"Young," Flow said walking up to us.

"What's good, Unc?" I greeted him as I always had. He wasn't my uncle, but the name showed the respect I had for him. Flow was the one that taught me and Noble everything about the streets.

"Look at you," he said, standing back and looking at me from head to toe. "You make an OG proud," he said, embracing me with a hug.

"This my boy Jar," I said introducing them.

"Why he look like he ready to kill a nigga?" Flow asked me while staring at Jar.

I laughed. "He mad because his sister be freaking me."

"Man, chill out with that shit," Jar said angrily. Flow and I laughed. Jar knew I was just bullshitting with him. He knew how much I cared about Amoy.

"What up?" Flow asked, holding his hand out to shake Jar's hand. Jar respectfully shook his hand.

"So, what's going on young? What kind of questions you need answers to?" he asked while taking a seat between us.

"My father," I said, looking at him.

"I knew this day would come," he said, shaking his head. "I don't know much, young, but I'll tell you whatever I can."

I told him everything about the letter my mom left me. He was shocked to find out Jar was the son of the couple my father killed and more shocked to find out we were friends.

"Damn, no wonder he was acting like he was losing his damn mind before the accident. They had him in a no-win situation. Only thing I can tell y'all, he drove for a company called Fast Way Trucking. Your father was a gambler not a drug head. He borrowed money from me but always paid me back. Something tells me this was a setup, but I don't know why. Young, get in touch with Stanley. He and your father was very close. He just got out of the state pen. So, you might find him in Lakeland. Check the old club called Three Oaks. Somebody might can tell you where to find him," he informed us.

"Thanks, Unc. Next visit will be more social," I said giving him a hug.

"Sorry that happened to your parents. Shit, I had just started to cop from him," Flow said to Jar. Jar nodded his head and shook Flow's hand.

*****

Lakeland, GA

Lakeland was a small town not too far from Valdosta. There was only one small club there, so it wasn't hard to find. By the time I had reached the age to go to the club, it wasn't hitting like it was when my father hung out there. Small town folks weren't too friendly with strangers, and Jar and I rolling up to the club in Jar's Maybach only made us more suspicious. Niggas were giving us the side eye.

"We toting?" Jar asked as we made our way to the front door of the club.

"Yea," I said, opening the door. The outside of the club didn't do the inside justice. It wasn't anything fancy, but it was nice. A few dudes played pool but kept their eyes on us while the females eyed us and whispered to each other. We took a seat at the bar.

"Ain't no old men here. And I ain't got time to get friendly with folks to find out where he at," Jar said, looking around the place.

He stood up, pulled out his gun, and shot in the ceiling of the club two times. A few females flew out the door with the speed of lightning. Niggas stood still with fear plastered on their faces.

"What da fuck?" I barked, standing up beside him.

"Listen up! We ain't here for trouble. We just looking for an old head named Stanley. Point us in his direction and we'll be on our way," Jar shouted.

"Man, you sound like you in some damn western movie," I said.

"You said this was a country ass town, so I assumed that's how they talk 'round these parts," Jar said.

"If you looking for me, all you had to do was ask for me. I ain't hard to find and I damn sho ain't hiding from no city niggas," a raspy voice said from behind us. I turned around to stare into the barrel of a sawed off shotgun. I tapped Jar to get him to turn around.

"Nice to meet you partner," he said smiling at the man. I shook my head. This nigga was crazy.

"What da fuck you want with me?" The man that I assumed was Stanley asked. The only thing I knew about Stanley was that he came to the house with my old man a few times. If he had anything to do with what happened to my old man and Amoy's parents, he'd be dead before Jar and I left.

Me and Jar turned around again when we heard a couple of guns cock.

"Oh, y'all wanna get brave and pull out guns now. Who wanna shoot me?" Jar asked, walking up to a short, skinny dude. I could see the gun shaking in his hand.

"You wanna have a show down?" Jar asked.

"Man, chill out. We came here to get information; don't add to your damn body count," I told him. He stared the guy down for a few minutes before walking away.

Stanley placed his shotgun on the table as Jar and I sat back down. He pulled out three shot glasses from under the bar and poured us shots of Black Velvet. I chuckled because I remembered my old man drinking that type of liquor. He gulped his down and poured himself another one. Jar and I just sat and stared at the glass of poison. He gulped down the glasses he poured for us.

"Y'all fancy city boys want Hennessy I guess," he said looking at us. We laughed, because he was right.

He stared at me for a few seconds. "Dachon Knight. I never thought you would live to be this age. You had a death wish on the streets."

"No disrespect but I don't have time to reminisce. I need answers about my father's death," I said. He glanced at Jar. "Whatever you gotta say, you can say it in front of him."

"Ask yo questions. I ain't got shit to hide," he said.

"How long was my father trafficking for that company he worked for?" I asked, leaning back in the seat.

"Shit son, it was practically since day one. That was why they hired him. First it was small jobs; then he started getting bigger and farther trips. I started to worry for him. The weight he was carrying was going to lock him up for life or send him to an early grave," he said.

"Are they still in business?" I asked.

"I don't know. After that happened with your father, I kinda kept to myself for a while," he said solemnly.

"Did you know?" I asked.

"Did I know what?" he asked curiously.

"That the accident was intentional," Jar chimed in.

"Nah, I ain't know nothing 'bout that," he said. No wonder the nigga never had luck at the card table; it was obvious he was lying.

"A'ight. This for the bullet holes this fool put in your ceiling," I said, placing a few bills on the bar.

We went to walk out the door, but a tall, skinny kid blocked us from walking out and stepped in the club.

"What up, Dak?" He said, holding out his hand for me to dap him. I didn't have a clue who he was.

"And who you?" I asked.

"It's me. Buckethead. You used to fuck with my sister, Lynette, a few years ago," he said.

I laughed. "Oh shit, nigga, yo body caught up with yo head." He laughed with me.

Lynette was from Lakeland but always came to the clubs in Valdosta. We kicked it for a while, but it was on a fun level. She wasn't 'bout shit, and she knew I wasn't shit for her, so we just fucked when we hooked up. Buckethead was a kid then; he looked to be about sixteen years old now.

"How old yo ass now?" I asked.

"Shit seventeen," he said smiling. Stanley stepped from around the bar and walked out the club.

Buckethead filled me in on what was going on with him. It touched my heart when he told me Lynette was killed in a drive by. She was fucking with a drug dealer and was caught up at the wrong place at the wrong time. In better news, Buckethead was one of the top scouts in Georgia as a basketball player.

"If you got all this going for you, why you out here hustling?" Jar asked.

"Who said I was hustling?" Buckethead asked.

Jar chuckled. "I can spot a corner boy anywhere?"

"A nigga gotta live and eat until I make it big. But on another note, y'all walk out that door, y'all gon' have bullet holes in y'all's body. Don't let these small town niggas fool you. They'll rock y'all asses to sleep," Buckethead told us.

"So we gotta shoot our way outta here?" Jar asked ready to dead some niggas.

"Nah, gimme a minute. I'll set shit straight for y'all," Buckethead said. He walked out of the club.

"You know that nigga lying, right?" Jar asked referring to Stanley.

"Yea, we'll catch him alone. Can't do shit here with all these witnesses," I told him. A few minutes later, Buckethead came back inside the club to let us know everyone was on chill.

"Leave the streets alone and put that energy into your future, man. Make something out of yourself for your mom and yo lil sister," I told him.

"Coming from two black dudes that rode up in a Maybach. What y'all do for a living?" He asked glancing at Jar and me.

"Stay out grown folks' business," Jar told him. Buckethead laughed.

I made a deal with him to follow Stanley when he closed the club. I would pay him good if he came through with the information tonight. He informed me that Stanley didn't own the club. He worked there to make a little change to support his habit. I knew he'd be looking for the dope man to spend the bills I gave him.

A Few Hours Later

Buckethead hit me up while we were at my house in Valdosta. Jar and I hopped in his car and drove the twenty minutes to meet up with him. He was standing on the corner of a fenced in trailer park.

"He still in there. Them fools be letting them get lit in the trailer," he answered.

"Didn't I tell you to leave that shit alone," I asked, looking at his backpack. I knew he had some product in it.

"Yea but Dak, I gotta eat. Moms barely can feed herself and my sister. She's not making enough to do it all working at the convenience store." He sounded defeated. "But I'm not hustling like that too much. I'm mostly making drops or posted out here looking out."

"Nah nigga, that shit ends today. I asked Flow about you, and he said you going big if you stay out of trouble. You have an opportunity to get out this shit. A black man with a chance to get out of the hood and make millions. Do you know how fucking rare that is? Don't let these streets take that from you," I pleaded.

"I feel ya, Dak, but shit I need to eat to stay focused. It's not like I'm out here doing this shit to buy clothes, shoes, and hoes. I'm doing this shit to maintain my stamina for the court. A brother can't keep his grades up on an empty stomach. My head on straight, Dak, for real. I just gotta do this for now," he explained desperately.

I pulled out my wallet. "From this point on, I don't want to hear anyone tell me they seen you posted up out here. I don't want to find out you making drops. I don't want you smoking or dealing any fucking drugs. Those lazy fools wanna make money sitting in the apartment getting high off their own product. They'll never come up. You take this and go stock your mom's fridge. I'll have someone stock the fridge for you every two weeks. This isn't a loan; I don't expect a damn thing for this. I only ask you to take advantage of the gift you've been blessed with," I said, handing him a wad of money.

He looked down at the wad in my hand. "Dak, our fridge don't hold that much food."

I laughed. "Go buy your little sister and Mama something nice with what's left."

"Dak, how I'm going to explain this to my mom's? She already be tripping about me out here doing this," he asked.

"Good for her. I'll talk with her before I leave. This isn't charity. This isn't an investment. You are my people. If I see where I can help a young brother have a future, I will do whatever I can. As long as he's trying to help himself. With that being said, there's one more rule for you to follow," I said.

"Stay away from anything that can get you into trouble. I mean girls, friends, enemies. If that shit not benefiting where you trying to go, leave that shit in the past. Don't take shit from anyone. Leeches see you on a come up, and they will consider you an investment. Don't take a damn candy bar from anyone. If you need anything, you got my number. Even if it's just to vent your frustration. Hell, if you need a break from all of this, holla at me. I know how this type of environment can break someone's spirit. I've lived this life. It's hard. Stay focused, stay hungry. You hear me?" I pleaded hoping he was listening to me.

"Thanks Dak. I know you real with this you telling me. I do want out this environment. I want my family to have better than this. I gotcha," he said, taking the money and giving me a brotherly hug.

"There go yo boy. He lit," Jar said.

I turned around to see Stanley wobbling down the three steps.

"Good looking. Now, get your ass off these corners," I said to Buckethead, walking away. I looked back and Buckethead was walking away from us.

"Don't you dare try to run," I said as Stanley looked at me with wide eyes.

"Dachon, I'm sorry for taking yo money. I'll pay you back. Better yet I got something better for you," he said terrified, backing up as I approached him.

"It better be worth it or you dead?" I asked, standing over him.

He informed me that a couple of dudes came to the club after we left and asked questions about me and Jar's visit. Stanley said they were going to kill him, so he told them about our visit.

"Your father was gambling heavy. He was hauling a load of product and stopped at a casino and met some female. To make a long story short, she had to set him up, because he was jacked that night. So, he owed them for what was stolen. That's when they blackmailed him to do what they needed done," he informed us.

"Who da fuck was they?" I asked.

He shook his head. "I never met them; I only know what your old man told me."

Before me or Stanley knew what happened, a fist was rammed into his face. I stood back and watched Jar beat him unconscious. I understood Jar's anger. He was furious because Stanley had this information but never spoke up. Plus, he lied to us when we initially asked him. Jar pulled out his gun ready to put a bullet in Stanley's head.

"You can't kill him. This a small town, and murders don't happen every day around here. Too many niggas seen our faces," I warned him. Jar ignored me and cocked his gun. The only thing that saved Stanley's life was a car coming up the road. We hopped back in Jar's vehicle and pulled off.

When we got back to my house, Jar was ready to leave. His anger was burning like a raging fire. I decided to stay a few days, so I text Amoy.

I love you

Come spend some time with me

It didn't take her long to text me back.

I love you too

I'll leave first thing in the morning

I texted her back to give here my location and to tell her to drive safe. Jar was headed back home first thing in the morning. He said he was going to try to find out who his father's connect was. Aunt Belle was the only one that had that information, and she wasn't sharing it with Jar because she was worried he would cut her out. Maybe she'd give him the information if she knew why he needed to know now.

Valdosta, GA

Amoy

As soon as I saw daylight, I got on the road. I was so relieved and happy to know that Dachon wanted to see me. I thought I had ruined things between us. Promising myself to trust him with my heart was hard, but I was going to try. He gave me a happiness that I had only seen between my parents. I wanted to live my life feeling that kind of love. The only way that was going to happen was to risk loving someone as much as I wanted to be loved. When I pulled into Dachon's driveway, he met me at the car and opened my driver's door. He didn't have on a shirt, so his chiseled abs were on display. His basketball shorts hung low, and his dick print was too obvious.

"Thanks for coming," he said, helping me out of the car.

I smiled. "Thanks for inviting me." I followed Dachon into the house; he carried my bag upstairs to the bedroom.

"You tired?" he asked as I flopped down on the bed.

"No, I'm hungry," I told him.

He walked over and sat in the big recliner in the corner of the bedroom. I became uncomfortable as he sat there staring at me. His stares always made me feel like he could read my mind and heart. Chills started traveling through my body as his eyes penetrated me. I looked away to break the hold he had on me.

"Look at me, Amoy," he said. His tone was seductive and demanding at the same time. I looked into his eyes, giving him my attention.

"I wanted to break you from that coldness that protected you. My goal was to prove to you that I could fuck you just like any other female, but it didn't happen that way. You're not as cold or tough as you portray yourself to be. There's a softness inside of you that pulled me in. I didn't want to fall for you no more than you wanted to fall for me, but it happened. I love you, but if trusting me is always going to be an issue for you this will never work," he stated.

"Do you really love me?" I asked nervously.

"I wouldn't say no shit like that unless I meant it. I don't have to tell you I love you to fuck you. I've already accomplished that," he said.

"Fuck you, Dachon," I stated angrily.

He laughed. "I'm only telling the truth, but I'm not fucking you anymore."

"What?" I asked confused. I knew this nigga didn't make me drive almost four hours to break things off with me again.

He smiled. "I'm making love to you now."

I giggled. "That's so damn corny. I love you too. I'm sorry for not believing your intensions. I want this to work between us, but I'm going to be honest with you, I don't want Lisa working with you. I don't trust her."

"It's not her that you have to trust. It's me," he told me.

"You've been acting so distant towards me. I thought you had started things up with her again," I confessed.

"I would never do anything to intentionally hurt you. I just ask you to give me a little time. There's some things I'm working through, and I need your patience and understanding," he said.

"Ok," I replied. Both of us were still dealing with the revelation of his father killing my parents. It affected him as much as it did me.

"Now, take off yo clothes," he said pulling his one-eyed monster from his shorts.

I smiled bashfully at him but started removing my clothes. He watched and stroked up and down his shaft. After removing my clothes and shoes, I walked over to him. Kneeling between his open legs, I wrapped his hard member in my hand. He released a low groan as my tongue stroked over the crown; I could feel his rod jump in my hand. I licked and sucked on the mushroom shaped head, letting my saliva slide down his shaft. My hand stroked up and down while my mouth started to suck him in and out. Taking deep breaths and strokes I could feel his crown hitting the back of my throat. His groans and grunts became louder as he pulsated inside my mouth. Saliva spilled from my mouth causing slurping sounds to echo through the room. My free hand fondled his wet balls and I tasted the precum that oozed from him. The sweet milky taste made me moan. The vibrations from my moans must've been too much for him. He yanked my head away to stop me.

"Fuck!" he said, standing up. When I stood up, he lifted me up by my ass cheeks wrapping my legs around his waist. "How you want it?"

His tongue licked and sucked all over my neck making me twirl and thrust my hips. I was eager to have him inside me. "Hard and rough," I moaned.

He carried me to the bed and laid me down. I positioned myself on all fours after he instructed me to turn over. I looked back at him and smiled as I spread my legs wider. He massaged my ass cheeks before pulling me closer to the edge of the bed. The palm of his hand pressed down in the center of my lower back causing my upper body to lay flat against the mattress. My ass was in the air leaving my soaking wet pussy on display for him. My body shivered and quaked as his tongue licked from between my ass cheeks to my dripping pussy. With his tongue devouring me and his finger assaulting my swollen clit, I was going insane. I cried out his name and pleaded for mercy. He didn't let up until my creamy juices were dripping from his goatee.

Without giving me a chance to catch my breath, he stood up and rammed his brick hard dick inside of me. I tried to cry out in pain and pleasure, but my cries got stuck in my throat. With my mouth wide open, I took everything he gave me. I could feel his dick spreading inside me and throbbing against my wet walls. My juices spilled down my inner thighs and splashed against the base of his shaft. His fingers dug into my ass cheeks as he slammed me against him. My ass cheeks jiggled like Jell-O on every stroke. My cries and his groans sounded like a horrible duet with the splashing of my juices and clapping of my ass as the music. I was coming back to back but requesting more. He gave me everything I begged for and more. When he slid his thumb inside my ass, I lost my mind. My pussy walls squeezed around his shaft and I oozed creamed. My heart fluttered, my mouth watered, and I exploded.

"Mottthhhaaa Fuuuucccckk! Aaaaarrrggghhh!" He roared. I could feel him releasing inside of me. He collapsed on top of me causing me to lay flat on the bed.

Two Days Later

We spent my first day in Valdosta in the bed. Later that night, we surprised Nobles' parents with an impromptu visit. His father instantly fired up the grill and his mother prepared a feast for us. We had a great time with them, and later that night I had the opportunity to visit Noble's club. I had a great time, but I wished Cache could've been there to enjoy it with me.

Over the next two days, he took me to different places and shared memories of his childhood. I loved the small city but felt like there was limited recreation available. After enjoying ourselves for two days, I decided it was time to return home. We visited Nobles' parents and said our goodbyes before we headed home. Instead of taking the turn to get on the interstate, Dachon took a different road.

"Where are we going?" I asked.

"I need to make a quick stop," he answered.

I sat quietly until we pulled in front of a convenience store. When we walked inside, I was shocked to see a black woman working behind the counter. Most convenience stores were owned by Arabs. I know that sounds like a stereotype but it's the truth.

"Well, look who we have here, Mr. Tall, Dark and Handsome himself," the black lady from behind the counter said smiling at Dachon.

"What's good, Linda?" Dachon asked as we walked toward the counter. She leaned over the counter and hugged his neck.

"You know, surviving," she said, shrugging her shoulders.

"I wanted to come by and see you before I left. I saw Buckethead a couple of days ago," Dachon said smiling.

"Boy, you still calling my baby that shit? He hated that name but let you call him that because he liked you," she said laughing.

Dachon laughed. "His head caught up with his body though."

"Yea, now my boy is just as handsome as you," she said smiling at him.

"He told me about Lynette. I'm sorry for your loss, Linda. She was good people," Dachon said solemnly.

"Now I'm worried about him in the streets," she replied sadly.

"You don't have to worry about him on the corners anymore. He got a chance of surviving this shit," Dachon stated sincerely.

"I'm with you, Dachon. I am on him every day about staying out of trouble; I can only pray he's listening, but I doubt it. I came home yesterday to a fridge full of food, cabinets stocked with can goods, cereal and shit. I know where he's getting that money from," she said, shaking her head.

"I came by because he said you would bitch about the groceries not knowing where he got the money from. That money was clean; I put some bread in his hand yesterday. He was working the corner when I ran into him. I know you are a proud woman, Linda. I also know you are a great mom and doing the best you can. This isn't charity nor an investment into Buckethead's future. I just don't want him to fuck up his chance. He needs to keep his focus on school and ball. I'm going to have someone stock the fridge every two weeks for y'all. It'll most likely be Noble's mom or sister that will come by," Dachon explained.

She started to cry. Dachon stood there until she pulled herself together. I wiped a tear from my own cheek.

"I don't know what to say but thank you. You have no idea how much that means to me," she said touching his hand as it rested on the counter. He nodded his head.

"Who's this beauty you got with you?" she asked, smiling at me.

Dachon glanced at me. "Just some female I'm fucking." My mouth dropped in disbelief. I punched him in the arm as he laughed.

"Hi, nice to meet you. I'm Linda," she said, laughing and reaching to shake my hand.

"Nice to meet you as well; I'm Amoy," I said shaking her hand.

"There's one other thing, but I don't know for sure yet. I might have a three-bedroom apartment available for you guys. Put your phone number in here," he said, handing her his phone.

"Dak, even with your help with groceries, I still couldn't afford your apartments," she said.

"They're low-income apartments, Linda. They're just in a better neighborhood. We'll work something out if it's still available. If not, you'll be first on my list for the next one," he said smiling.

"Damn, you got him smiling and being all giving and shit. Hell, I used to wonder did the nigga have teeth," she said, looking at him laughing.

I laughed too. She was beautiful, but you could see that the stress was wearing her beautiful face down. She was a shade lighter than me and slender with a neat shape. She wore her hair in a low natural afro that fit her perfectly. She put her number in Dachon's phone and gave it back to him.

"Well, we gotta get out of here. I'll be in touch with you by the end of the week," he said, reaching over the counter and giving her a hug.

"It was nice to meet you," I said smiling. She smiled back.

I could only stare at him when we got in the car. He did the most thoughtful thing for someone, and it wasn't beneficial to him in any way.

"What?" he asked, staring back at me.

"I love you," I said smiling at him.

He chuckled and shook his head. "Corny ass shit." I laughed.

Two Weeks Later

Cache

I ignored Mama's umpteenth phone call. I knew she was only calling to be nosey about my pregnancy. Stephanie told me she accidently told her. I loved Stephanie but she couldn't hold water. I didn't care if Mama knew, but I didn't want to share this experience with her. She could never be a grandmother to my child after walking out of my life.

"You ain't gon' answer that?" Noble asked as we lay in his bed.

"No," I said, straddling his lap.

My ankle healed fast because it was only a minor sprain. Noble was being overprotective and wouldn't have sex until he felt I was ready. My hormones were a raging mess and I was horny. He looked up at me and smiled giving me the okay to take what I wanted. Just as I was getting ready to pull his hard dick from his boxers, his phone rang. I rolled my eyes and climbed off him when I saw Dinah's name. She called him nonstop every hour of the day with her complaints, needs, and wants.

"Hey Dinah," he said answering the call on speaker phone.

"I'm still bleeding, and I don't have any pads," she said with an attitude.

"A'ight. I'll be over in about an hour. You need anything else?" he asked nicely.

"If you don't mind, can you bring me something to eat. Our baby is as greedy as me. She sucks bottle after bottle," Dinah said.

He laughed. "Yea, yo ass always did love to eat. I'll bring something."

"Thanks Noble. You've really been a big help, and it's okay if you wanna bring Cache to see our baby," Dinah said. That nearly knocked the breath out of me. She was adamant that she didn't want me nowhere near their child.

"What she doing?" Noble asked smiling.

"She's asleep right now. I enjoy these few moments of solitude," Dinah said.

"A'ight. I'll be there in a few," he said ending the call.

"You sound like a family man," I said sadly. I wanted to be understanding of the situation, but it was hard.

"Don't start that shit, Cache," he said getting off the bed.

"You spend more time with her than you do with me since the baby's here. How da fuck am I supposed to feel?" I said angrily.

"I'm spending time with my child not her. That's some shit you gon' have to understand," he said.

"I see what's happening. You are not only developing a bond with the baby; you're also getting close to Dinah again. That's just what she wanted. The bitch just wants me to come over so she can rub the baby in my face. I'll pass," I said. I stood there with my arms folded waiting for him to beg me to go with him.

"Fine," he said. My mouth dropped as he put on his clothes.

"So, you just gon' leave just like that?" I asked angrily.

"Yea, you coming or not. I'm just trying to be as nice as possible to Dinah so she will agree to the blood test.

Or let me bring the baby home with me, so I can do one of those home tests. So what's it going to be?" he said.

I stood silent a few seconds. "I'm going."

"That's what da fuck I thought. Now hurry up so we can get back home, so I can tear the lining out that pussy," he said, walking over and smacking me on the ass. I giggled.

*****

When we got to Dinah's house, a Latina with a mean mug on her face opened the door. She walked away leaving the door open without speaking. Noble took my hand and we walked inside. He had set Dinah up in a nice ass apartment. It was just as big as mine, but the place was a mess. I had to remember Dinah was caring for a newborn. She didn't have time to clean, take care of herself, and the baby, because she wasn't quite healed. I placed the bag of pads on the center table. Noble sat the Wing Stop bag on the table.

"Who is this?" the Latina asked. She sat down, crossed her legs, and lit a cigarette.

"Hi, I'm Cache. You must be Dinah's mom. It's nice to meet you," I lied politely.

"No need to lie. Ain't shit nice about this situation. This nigga got my daughter pregnant and abandoned her," she said, rolling her eyes at me.

"Penelope, put that shit out around the baby," Noble demanded. She sucked her teeth and dropped the cigarette in a soda can. She grabbed the Wing Stop bag off the table and started eating Dinah's food.

"You can eat my shit, but couldn't go to the store for me?" Dinah asked angrily.

"I ain't yo baby daddy. That's his job," Penelope replied.

As they bickered back and forth, my eyes zeroed in on the beautiful baby girl lying in the bassinet. Noble hadn't fully accepted the baby as his, but he made sure Dinah and the baby had everything they needed. Since Noble rejected her offer to help name the baby, Dinah named her Stella. *A Streetcar Named Desire* was her favorite movie. At least that's what Noble told me. Stella had a head full of jet-black, curly hair. Stella started to wake up and cry, and I so desperately wanted to pick her up but didn't want to overstep my boundaries. My heart melted when Noble picked her up, and she instantly stopped whining. He held her so perfectly.

"Hold her a minute," he said, passing Stella to me. I immediately shook my head, but he had placed her in my arms. She was angelic. Her eyes were jet-black and as round as a full moon.

"Shut da fuck up!" Noble barked at Dinah and Penelope. Both nearly jumped out their skin.

"Get out! Only reason you came here was to get money from me. I don't have shit to give you," Dinah said to Penelope.

"Yo stupid ass got pregnant from a nigga that don't want you or the baby. That's why you broke now," Penelope said, standing up. I felt sorry for Dinah. She truly had no one to help her with Stella, but Noble. Dinah flopped down on the sofa crying, and Penelope walked out the apartment. Noble pulled out his phone and walked out of the living room. Dinah stopped crying and looked up at me holding her baby.

"I'm sorry. Noble didn't want to yell while holding her, so he gave her to me," I explained.

"I'm so tired. I just need a break," she said. She looked worn out and stressed.

Noble came back into the living room. "Pack some things. Y'all going to stay with Ma and Pops until you heal. We taking the paternity test in three days while you there. I don't want to hear shit about it, Dinah. I need to know if I'm her father. You and Stella need to know for sure. It ain't fair to anyone of us to not be sure."

Dinah nodded her head. Noble reached for Stella, but I didn't want to let her go. I sat and held her until she fell back to sleep.

Three Days Later

Noble was still in Valdosta getting Dinah situated and handling business. I didn't know how I felt about him spending so much time with Dinah, but I had to trust him. The funny thing was I thought I wanted Stella to be his. That beautiful little baby deserved to be in a loving family, not a family like Penelope's. She didn't care about her grandchild. Her only concern was what she could get from Dinah and Noble.

I was lounging in my den eating ice cream when my doorbell rang. It had to be Amoy, because she was the only person that would come to my place unannounced. I made my way to the door and was shocked to see my mother standing on the other side. I rolled my eyes at her and stood there.

"Aren't you going to invite me in, Catherine?" she asked.

"I told you my name is Cache," I said.

"Fine. May I please come in, Cache," she said. I stepped to the side to let her in. She followed me to the den where I sat back down and resumed eating my ice cream.

"Why have you been avoiding my calls?" she asked.

"Why did you abandon me for money?" I asked to taunt her.

"Stephanie told me about the pregnancy. Congratulations. You will be a wonderful mother. I hope it's the young man you brought to dinner. He's going to be very rich one day," she said smiling as she sat down.

"Is that all you damn think about...money? I wouldn't care if he didn't become rich. He's a good man and provider like my father was. That's all that matters to me," I said furiously.

"I just want the best for you and my grandchild. What's wrong with that?" she asked.

I just shook my head, because she truly has no clue of the mental and emotional damage she caused me, or she just didn't give a damn.

"You won't have the opportunity to spoil my baby. I don't want you or your family near my child," I told her.

"I've been attending the sessions with the psychiatrist like you requested. It's time we start trying to mend our relationship," she said.

"Before we can mend our relationship, you need to mend yourself just like I need to work on me," I said.

"When was the last time you saw your father? Do you talk to him like this?" she asked.

"Are you serious? My father has been there for me my entire life. My stepmom treats me more like a daughter than you do. I call my father every day to let him know how much I love and appreciate him," I spewed at her.

"Cather... I mean Cache, I'm trying. You will never understand how hard it was to walk away from my family," she stressed.

"If this is what you call trying...just don't. All this is pointless. You are trying to get me to understand why you left me for money. There is no explanation for abandoning your child. What is it about that you don't understand?" I asked her with an agitated tone.

"If I had taken you with me, they would've isolated you...made you feel unwanted. I just couldn't watch them do that to you," she exclaimed.

"So, it was okay for you to do that to me, but not them? Do you actually hear yourself when you speak this nonsense?" I asked, standing up.

"Of course not. I just knew you would be better off with him." She continued with her logic.

"Or, why not choose to stay with your family through the hard times instead of running back to your racist parents for their money?" I asked, looking down at her.

"You don't understand," she said, shaking her head.

"You are right, I don't. So here's what's going to happen from this point on, I don't give a damn if you go to the sessions. I don't want to hear from you until you are ready to accept full responsibility for your actions without excuses. Until you are ready to waltz my black ass into your racist parents' home as your daughter that you will no longer deny publicly, I want you out of my life," I stated firmly.

Noble walked into the den. I immediately wipe a tear that was sitting on my cheek. I was so frustrated with her; I didn't hear him enter the front door.

"What's wrong?" he asked, walking over to me.

"Nothing baby, my mother was just leaving," I said glancing at her.

She stood up, walked past Noble, then she looked back at me. "I'm sorry, Cache. Just give me time, please."

"No, I've given you enough time. I'm done," I told her.

She dropped her head and walked toward the front door. My eyes closed as I took a deep breath to control my emotions. Noble's arms wrapped around me and he held me tight. I buried my face in his chest and let out a much-needed cry. He carried me in his arms to the bedroom where we lay quietly.

"I'm glad you're back. My stepmom brought too much food over here. Are you hungry?" I said laughing.

"Hell yea," he said, rubbing his stomach.

I prepared our food, and we sat at the table talking and laughing. He told me the paternity test was completed and the results would take a couple of weeks. I felt relieved knowing Stella was going to get love from his parents while they are there.

Six Weeks Later

Noble

I was at my sports bar going over paperwork before it opened. My management team was the best so, outside of doing paperwork, I didn't have to worry about spending much time at the bar.

Dinah returned back to Atlanta a week ago, so she allowed me and Cache to keep Stella sometimes when she wanted to go out. My plan for the weekend was to enjoy some alone time with Cache since we had kept Stella for Dinah last weekend to give her a break. She had been very cooperative and generous about Stella spending time with us. Still, every day I anxiously checked the mail waiting for the paternity test results.

Whenever I looked at Stella, I didn't see any resemblance of myself. I didn't feel the connection that I thought I should as her father. Cache and I had numerous arguments about my distance toward Stella. We had fallen in love with Stella, but Cache had developed a motherly bond with her. It was going to break her heart if we had to walk away from her. I didn't want to feel the pain of having to break a bond with the beautiful little girl, but I knew I would handle it better than Cache. Dinah using Cache's love for Stella was even more reason for a paternity test. I know Dinah was only using Cache to enjoy her freedom.

"Hey," Cache said walking into the office. She had called me and said she would be stopping by after her last class. Cache was finally starting to show. Her beautiful face was getting round, her belly was protruding, and she had what they called the pregnancy glow. Plus, her hair was growing like crazy. When I met her, it stopped at her neck; now it was almost touching her shoulders.

"I won't be much longer," I said. She walked over and kissed me softly on my lips before sitting on the love seat on the other side of the room. I could tell something was bothering her.

"What's wrong?" I asked.

"Nothing," she said.

"Don't lie, Cache," I said staring at her.

She took a deep breath. "My mother keeps calling and texting me. I just want to forget that part of my life. Being around her makes me remember how low I felt about myself at one time. It brings back so much hurt and anger."

"Do you love her?" I asked.

"That's what makes me so mad. After what she did, I still love her," she said. I walked over and sat down beside her.

"It's okay to love someone that hurt you. It's only wrong when you give them the power to control your happiness. Forgiving her doesn't mean you have to allow her back into your life. How about you work on truly forgiving her. Then, we'll go from there," I suggested.

"I've already tried to forgive her," she said.

"Nah, you've used the opportunity to torture her. You want her to hurt as much as she hurt you," I told her.

"That's true but it's not even fun because she acts as if she doesn't care," she said.

"I think she does, but she doesn't know how to reach you," I told her.

"I'll try," she said.

She straddled my lap and bit softly on my bottom lip before sliding her tongue in my mouth. I sucked on her tongue before sliding mine in her mouth. My hands slid under her jean skirt, and I could feel the warmth coming from her pussy. Her panties were soaked. I pushed her skirt up to her waist and slipped my fingers inside her panties. My fingers slid between her wet fold as our tongue kiss got deeper. When I slipped two fingers inside her drenched tunnel, she started winding her hips.

"You so damn wet," I moaned, breaking our kiss. I started licking and sucking on her neck as I poked and toyed with her g-spot. She threw her head back and started riding my fingers.

"Aaahhh yeesss!" She cried out gushing her sweet juices on my hand.

I pulled my fingers from her and quickly pulled my brick hard dick from my pants. Cache didn't waste time mounting my pole. I slapped both her ass cheeks and palmed them like a basketball. She bounced up and down splattering her juicy essences between us. Her walls were slippery, juicy, and tight. I let her ass go and massaged her full breasts. I sucked, licked and nibbled on her breasts and nipples as she rode my dick.

"Oooh shit! I'm bout to come again!" She screamed. I gripped her around the waist and started thrusting my dick deep inside her. My crown was torturing her spot as she showered my throbbing dick with her juices. Her body trembled as her orgasm ripped through her.

"Keep riding this dick," I demanded. I slid my hand down and played with her sensitive clit. She was going crazy. She twirled and grinded on me making my dick harder as my dick spread inside her. Her ass cheeks slapped against my thighs.

"Fuck! This pussy good!" I barked feeling myself getting ready to come. It only took a couple more bounces on my dick before I was unloading inside of her.

*****

When we got to my house, we went upstairs to take a shower. After the shower, Cache went downstairs to get a snack. I heard her calling my name, so I hurried downstairs. Cache was standing in the kitchen holding an envelope. I knew what it was, but I was still shocked to actually have the results.

"I decided to check the mail while I was down here," she said staring at me. I walked over and took the envelope from Cache's hand and started to open it.

"Baby stop!" She yelped.

"What's wrong?" I asked concerned.

"We need to discuss this first," Cache said, walking out of the kitchen.

"Baby, we already have…I thought," I said, following her to the den.

"The issue isn't if she is yours. The issue is what if she isn't. Noble, you can't say you and your family haven't developed feelings for that beautiful little girl. It would be hard not to," she stated while sitting on the sofa.

"Yea, I have but not as much as you. I've discussed all this with my parents, and we've prepared for either outcome. You act like you want her to be mine." I was puzzled by her stance on this topic.

"You think Stella will be okay if you're not her father?" she questioned.

"We can always check in on Stella to make sure Dinah is being a good mother," I assured her.

Cache took a deep breath. "Ok, open it."

I slowly opened the envelop. I looked up at Cache before unfolding the results, and she urged me to open the letter with her eyes, so I did. I didn't know how to feel about the results I was reading. I wanted to be angry, but I felt a bit of disappointment.

"What does it say?" Cache asked nervously.

I looked up at her. "She's not mine."

Cache didn't have to tell me how she felt. I could see the hurt and disappointment on her face. This was the reason I didn't want to get emotionally attached to Stella before knowing if she was mine. Before Cache could respond to the results, my phone rang, and Dinah's number was on the screen. I assumed she must've gotten the results today as well. I answered the phone with her on speakerphone.

"I texted you two hours ago. She won't stop crying," Dinah said sounding defeated.

"Have you changed and fed her?" I asked.

"Of course I have. I know how to take care of my damn child. I don't want to talk to your insensitive ass. Where's Cache?" Dinah asked infuriated.

"I'm right here. Have her bowels moved today? Does she have a fever?" Cache asked.

"She already boo-booed. I don't know if she has a fever. I haven't slept in over twenty-four hours. Can you please just come get her for a little while?" Dinah asked Cache.

Cache looked at me to see my expression. That was a no go. We had to cut our ties with Dinah.

"Nah, but we'll come over. We need to talk," I said before ending the call.

"What if she's really sick?" Cache asked concerned.

"That's why we going over there. We'll make sure she's okay. After that, we'll discuss the results with Dinah. Now, come on," I told her.

Dachon

T hings had been going great between Amoy and me. If she wasn't sleeping at my house, I was at her spot. Even though things were great, I still felt guilty for keeping the secret about our parents from her. It was time for me to tell her the truth. Jar and I weren't getting any information on why my old man was hired to kill their parents. Every small lead we got led to a dead end.

Jar and Aunt Belle had come to an agreement, so the war was off. Reluctantly, she gave him the majority of the territory. She didn't have much of a choice because Jar and Noble were pushing her out of the game day by day, but I was relieved that the family feud over. She couldn't stand the sight of me and I understood why, so I made myself scarce whenever she was around.

Tonight, Amoy was cooking dinner for everyone at her house. She even invited Nova, and she was pissed off because Jar wasn't there. She felt like Nova was perfect for Jar. I didn't see it, because Jar wasn't stable enough to handle someone like Nova. Her energy was peaceful and unproblematic while Jar was a raging bull.

We had finished dinner and we were drinking and having a few laughs. It was good to relax and spend time with Noble and Cache. All our lives seemed to be so busy that we didn't have much time for each other.

Jar finally joined us, but I could tell something was on his mind. When Amoy started to give him hell about being late, he gave her a look that told her to let it go. He was so wrapped in his thoughts that he didn't pay Nova any attention until she approached him.

"Wanna drink my liquid?" she asked him. Everyone laughed. The question was completely innocent, but it sounded erotic as fuck. Nova had made some liquid marijuana, which none of us were willing to try, but we smoked her high-quality weed. Cache was the only sober one there. We were all high as hell.

"What da fuck?" Jar asked, looking around for an explanation.

She took him by the hand and led him into the kitchen. When they came back into the room, Jar was much more relaxed. There was a strong connection between he and Nova, but I didn't think he was ready to explore what they had. Watching them interact was weird, because it seemed innocent but erotic at the same time.

As the night went on, everyone came down from their high. After Noble and Cache left, the rest of us watched a movie. Nova fell asleep cuddled up under Jar, and Amoy had her head in my lap snoring like a cub.

"Better be careful with that. She might lock you down," I told Jar.

"Why da fuck she smell sweet all the damn time? That's the only reason I'm letting her lay on me," Jar said. I laughed.

"What was the look about when you came in the house?" I asked.

He carefully stood up and nodded for me to follow him. We walked out the kitchen door that led to the pool and sat at one of the two patio tables.

"The trucking company that your father worked for never closed down. It was renamed after it grew bigger," he said, playing on his phone.

"Do you know the name of the company?" I asked.

"Bro, the fucking company is owned by Eric's dad," Jar said passing me his cellphone. Eric was the square that Amoy called herself dating in an effort to not fall for me.

I was stunned. I looked up at Jar after viewing the information on the screen.

"It's time to make a visit to Williams' Trucking Service," Jar said looking at me.

The Next Day

I met Jar at his place so we could make a surprise visit at Eric's father's office. We were getting ready to leave when someone knocked on Jar's front door. He pulled out his phone and looked at the screen.

"Who da fuck?" he asked, making his way to the door. We pulled out our guns and I followed behind him. I didn't see who was on the screen, but I wanted to have Jar's back in case there was trouble. Fear didn't dwell inside of Jar as he opened the door without a care in the world. I knew the man standing on the other side of the door and wondered what the hell he was doing at Jar's house. His name was Juan Felipe. He was one of the biggest cocaine suppliers in Columbia. I didn't know him personally, but I had been in his presence a few times.

"Mr. Jarvis Alexandria, I heard you've been inquiring about me," he said.

"I know who da fuck you are, but I don't recall requesting your presence at my house nor me asking about you," Jar stated boldly.

"May I come in?" he asked.

"Not with them two big gorillas standing behind you," Jar told him.

Juan chuckled and ordered the men to stay outside. Jar stepped to the side to let Juan in and led us to his den. Juan walked to Jar's mini bar and poured himself a drink. He sat down and made himself comfortable like he was at home. Jar and I just stood there watching him.

"Word got back to me that you have been wanting to know your father's supplier. Now, you know," Juan said.

"You supplied my old man?" Jar asked surprised.

"Don't be so surprised. Your father was going to be a very powerful man. I don't supply small hustlers, but I saw something different in your father. I'm so sorry for his early demise. You are the spitting image of your father. He would be very proud of you. You're making major moves in the city; I guess you want me to supply you like I did your father," Juan said looking at Jar.

"I mean dat shit would be sweet, but that ain't why I was seeking my father's supplier," Jar informed him.

Juan gave Jar a curious look. "Explain."

"Did you know my father was murdered?" Jar asked.

Juan looked perplexed by the news. A man of his statue never showed discomfort. That was how I knew he was utterly shocked at Jar's revelation.

"Where did you get such information?" he asked.

"This man here is the son of the driver of the other vehicle. His mom left him a letter detailing what happened," Jar explained. He continued to tell Juan all the information we knew leading up to Jar getting shot. Juan sat there quietly, rubbing his jaw line.

"What are you going to do with this information?" he asked looking at both of us.

"I want whoever did this to pay for my parents' death," Jar stated sternly.

"What do you know about Reginald Williams?" I asked referring to Eric's father.

"Mr. Williams was highly upset because I chose to only supply your father in this area. After your father's death, I became his supplier. I didn't like some of his dealings, so I cut them off. After your father died, I chose to supply them again. I leave you with that bit of information." he said in his heavy accent standing up. He walked over and shook our hands; then we followed him to the front door. He turned to face us.

"If you haven't avenged your parents' death in a timely manner. I will seek my revenge for their dishonesty to me. One thing I value most in this world is the truth, and they didn't give me that. I will give you a month to handle this in your way. I do this because this vengeance is personal to you. But after that, it is a business vengeance for me. I will tell you to keep following your leads. You're heading in the right direction. Just be prepared for what you will find out. I did not know of this. I thought it was an accident. But now I see. They were brilliant with their plan," Juan warned us before walking out the front door.

"Do you feel he's not telling us everything?" I asked Jar.

"I know he wasn't. He said *they*," Jar said in deep thought. "You think he was in on it?" Jar asked looking at me.

"Nah, I've been in that man's presence a few times. I never seen him shook, but he was shook by that news. I think it's time to pay Mr. Williams a visit. We have a month to figure this shit out," I said. He nodded in agreement.

Later That Day

Jar and I were sitting in the parking lot waiting on the call. I answered my phone when it rang.

"Done," the caller said on the other end.

"Hold that shit. This can be a big come up for you if you handle this shit right," I advised him.

We had hijacked a truck full of drugs from Reginal that belonged to Juan.. We weren't worried about stealing from Juan. We could return them or let Jar and Noble. Juan would be extremely happy with how fast they pushed his product. After the phone call, we made our way inside the building.

"We're here to see Mr. Williams. Tell him he doesn't want to turn us away. That would be a bad move," Jar said. His tone was low and filled with malice.

The white reception quickly stood from her desk and rushed to Mr. Williams' office. We stayed standing waiting on her to return. I check to make sure my gun was secured in the back of my pants.

"He'll see you now," she said opening the door wide to let us enter.

Mr. Williams was pacing the floor while on the phone. He was a tall black man and reminded me of Don Cheadle. He immediately hung up and we casually sat in the two chairs in front of his desk. He finally sat down looking anxious.

"What can I do for you," he asked not really giving us much attention.

"It's more like what can I do for you," Jar said with a smile.

"Excuse me," he said glancing at us. He bore an irritated expression as if he had better things to do than to be playing games with us.

"I have your dope, motherfucker," Jar said with a scowl on his face.

"You son of a bitch!" Mr. Williams screamed standing and leaning over his desk.

"Calm down, we have a lot to discuss," Jar said, gesturing his hand for Reginald to have a seat.

"What the hell do you want from me? Look Jar, I see you have taken up with the wrong kind of associates. Your father would not approve of you getting caught up in the business," he said cutting his eyes at me.

"Did my father's name truly just roll off your snake ass tongue," Jar asked looking as if he was ready to blow. I only hoped he would control his temper. I knew he was strapped, and we didn't need any heat-of-the-moment reactions right now.

"I knew your father very well, and I know he wouldn't approve of this," he said as beads of sweat appeared on his forehead. Jar stood up, and I knew he was going for his gun.

"If I was you, I would chill with all that and just listen. I'm only here to make sure you stay alive," I said giving the nervous brother a sinister smile.

"We can make this easy or hard. It's your choice. I'm going to ask you some questions, and you *will* answer truthfully. It's your choice how this plays out," Jar said sitting back down and rubbing his jaw line.

"You have no idea whose shipment you are fucking playing with," Reginald said with a threatening tone.

"Oh I do; Juan Felipe," Jar said with a grin. Reginald was shocked to know we had that information.

"Oh now I see we have your attention," I said smiling at him.

"Why did you have my father and mother killed?" Jar asked staring Reginald in the eyes. Reginald was definitely not a poker player. He tried to show a shocked expression, but it looked completely fake.

"I have no idea what the hell you are talking about," he answered trying to seem clueless. In one quick motion, Jar had stuck a letter opener in the backside of Reginald's hand. Reginald let out a painful howl.

"Mothafucka shut up before I tell them to dump that truck," Jar warned him. Reginald flopped down in his seat trying to fight through the pain without crying out loud. Sweat started to pour from his face.

"Sir, is everything okay?" his receptionist asked while lightly knocking on the office door.

"Tell da bitch to go to lunch or something," Jar said. Reginald tried to sound as normal as possible as he assured her everything was okay and that she could leave for the day. His hand was still stuck to the table by the letter opener. Neither of us spoke until we heard the office door open and close signaling that she was gone.

Jar looked at me, "Make the call. Tell them to dump all that shit." I pulled out my phone and pretended to dial.

"Hold up! Wait a minute!" Reginald yelled. I stopped fake dialing and looked at Jar. He looked back at Reginald and pulled the letter opener from his hand causing blood to pour all over his desk. I walked over to the small mini bar and grabbed a towel for him to wrap his hand. He started pacing the floor.

"I don't have all fucking day," Jar said getting agitated with him.

Reginald started singing like a canary. "He took every fucking thing! I was cut out of the deal! We brought him in, and he snaked us," he hissed. "We all went in this together, but Juan cut us out. Your father became the main supplier…leaving us with nothing."

"Who the fuck is *we?*" Jar asked. Reginald stared Jar in the face. His facial expression was now calm.

"Oh son, I don't think you want to know the answer to that question," he replied while shaking his head from side to side.

"Mothafucka first of all, I'm not your bitch ass son! I'm not here to play guessing games with you. You killed my damn parents because you were fucking jealous because my dad hustled harder than you. Just like a bitch ass nigga. Now who the fuck else was involved in this?" Jar demanded to know.

Reginald walked over and stared Jar directly in the eyes.

"Belinda. It was all her idea. *Kill him and Juan will supply us again,*" he said mimicking her. "We wouldn't have to sex traffic anymore, and she would take over for your father," he said in a low and calm voice. He stayed in position staring Jar down. Before I could react, Jar had his gun to Reginald's head.

"You lying mothafucka!" Jar said still staring Reginald down. He knew he had Jar shook by mentioning Belinda. I didn't know who Belinda was, but she must have been someone important to Jar. I stood from my seat and touched Jar on his shoulder.

"You can't kill him here. The receptionist saw us," I reminded him. It was a constant task having to remind Jar to think before he reacted when he was angry. He didn't shoot Reginald, but the blow to his head with the butt of Jar's gun sounded painful. Jar pointed his gun at Reginald as he fell on the floor.

"You scream and I'll blow yo brains out," Jar warned Reginald. Blood leaked from his head. Reginald lay on the floor in a fetal position.

"She was the woman that set the trucker up. She fucked him and had us steal our own drugs from him. That's how we set him up to do what we needed done," he said looking at me and acknowledging that he knew who I was. He was too scared to move a muscle to wipe the blood that was pouring down his face.

Jar started pacing the floor, but then he stopped and faced Reginald. Reginald slowly and carefully pulled himself up off the floor and flopped down in his chair.

"Did you try to fucking kill us at the club?" he asked Reginald with a scowl on his face.

"No, I didn't know anything about that until after the incident. I'm innocent on that one," Reginald admitted.

"Let's get out of here," Jar said, walking toward the door.

"Jarvis, what about my shipment? You can't do this! You have no idea how much money is in there. That will be all our lives!" Reginald pleaded standing up from his chair.

Jar turned around, walked back over, and stood directly in Reginald's face. "So when you killed my father and mother, it was only business, right?" Jar asked tilting his head to the side.

"Never personal. Your father was a decent man," Reginald answered thinking Jar was trying to be understanding. But I had seen the look in a man's eyes who was plotting murder. Jar's eyes were no different, only more focused.

Jar placed a hand on Reginald's shoulder. "I'll be in touch about your shipment. Thanks for the information," Jar said with a sinister smile and turned to walk away.

Before opening the door, he spoke again. "And Reginald, if anything happens to any member of my family from this point on, you have no idea the kind of havoc I will bring to your life. And don't try to have anyone trailing me. That would not be a good idea. Just sit tight until you hear from me," Jar said, opening the door and walking out. I followed behind him.

Inside the car, Jar pulled out a burner phone from the glove compartment. After dialing a phone number he spoke.

"I have all the information from him I need. I will have your shipment back to you tomorrow. I will let you have the vengeance on this one, since it was only business. I will have the other vengeance. It's personal," Jar spoke into the phone. I could only assume he was talking to Juan.

"Yea, he thinks I'm going to return it to him. So, if you want you can still make him pay for the shipment. He doesn't want you to know it's been taken or why. A win for you," Jar said with a chuckle. "No, thank you, Juan," Jar said ending the call.

We rode in silence until we reached our homes. I could tell he was in deep thought, so I didn't ask the questions that I wanted the answers to.

"I need some time to sort this shit out in my head fam," he said when we pulled in his driveway. "Let me get back with you in a few hours," he said staring out the windshield window.

"Yea, I gotcha. Hit me up later." I gave him a handshake and exited the vehicle.

Something told me I needed to keep a close eye on Jar. His eyes craved murder and revenge. Normally I wouldn't have a problem with it, but something didn't sit right in my soul this time.

Amoy

"You like this, Aunt Belle?" I asked. She was going away for an extended vacation and I was helping her shop.

"Girl, I'm not getting all my ass in that," she said, looking at the dress.

"It's classy and sexy. Might come back with a young Jamaican and long plaits like Stella," I said jokingly.

"Chile, I don't need to go to Jamaica to be Stella. I fuck young niggas on American soil," she said boastfully.

"Ewww, Aunt Belle," I said turning my nose up at her. I laughed as she waved me off.

After we spent hours shopping, we made our way to the food court. I noticed she kept staring at me. Sometimes I hated looking at her, because she reminded me so much of my mother. Aunt Belle had a more edgy side to her. She loved the street life while Ma only wanted to be a wife and good mother. Her dreams were fulfilled before her life was taken. Aunt Belle finally broke her silence.

"I'm going to be gone for a while, Amoy. I want you to know I love you and your brother very much. Everything I did was to secure your future and your children's future. I wasn't perfect like your mother, but I did my best," she said sadly.

"I know, Aunt Belle. Me and Jar love and thank you for everything you did for us," I said graciously. She reached over and placed her hand on top of mine.

"I hope you find the happiness you want," she said smiling.

I laughed. "You're saying things like you aren't coming back. It's only for a few weeks. You'll be around to help me raise my babies."

Her softness turned ice cold. "I hope you aren't going to have kids with that boy. Your parents would turn over in their graves."

I didn't reply to her comment. She couldn't make me feel bad or guilty for loving Dachon anymore. What happened to our parents was horrible, but it wasn't his fault. I believed my parents would love Dachon. I know Daddy would, because he reminded me of him a lot. He liked to clown but could be distant and mean at times. My phone vibrated and I read Dachon's text.

I'm at your house and you're not here

I sent him a text to let him know I'd be there shortly.

*****

When I arrived at my house, Dachon was sitting in the den. The lights were off, and the sound of rain was playing over the surround sound. I walked over and straddled his lap. His rough hands caressed the side of my face before he pulled my face to his and gave me the softest, wettest, most sensual kiss that left my pussy throbbing and panties wet.

"I love you too," I said softly after our kiss ended.

"I wanna take you away for a little while," he said.

"Ok, when and where are we going. I need to put in a notice with my job. It's just an internship, but I have to be professional," I told him.

"You pick the place; I want to leave as soon as possible," he said.

"I wanna go to Brazil. Nova said it's so beautiful and peaceful," I told him.

"Let your job know you'll be leaving in a couple of days," he said.

I laughed. "I can't leave that soon. Especially since Nova quit. Now, I have to take up her slack. That girl is all over the place. She got her master's degree only to decide the corporate world isn't for her."

"I'm serious. See how quick you can take off," he said.

"Ok, I'll talk to my supervisor tomorrow. Why the urgency?" I asked.

"I just want some time with you away from everything and everybody," he replied.

"I'm going into the kitchen to cook my man a fat juicy steak and steak fries. Stay in here and relax," I said, getting off his lap.

It didn't take long to pan fry the T-bone steak and cook the fries. Dachon sat at the kitchen isle eating while I talked about the places Nova informed me of in Brazil. After eating his meal, Dachon made me his dessert on the kitchen isle. We fucked from the kitchen to my bedroom.

"Have you talked to Jar today. I've been trying to call him all day, but he's not answering. I need to get with him about the upcoming charity event he's hosting," I said. I was lying on his chest in the bed.

"I saw him earlier. We supposed to link up later. By the way, do you know anyone by the name Belinda?"

I laughed. "Yea, that's our aunt. Aunt Belle is the nickname Jar gave her years ago. Why?"

"I-I just asked. Heard Jar mention that name. Never heard him say the name before," he said. He tapped me on the ass and told me he needed to go check on something at the club. I didn't believe him, but I moved and let him up.

"I'll go with you," I said.

"Nah, stay here. It won't take long. And get that look off your face, Amoy. This business I'm going to handle," he said. I smiled and nodded my head.

After Dachon left, I ended up going through old pictures of my parents. There was an uneasy feeling inside me. I started to think about the conversation I had with Aunt Belle earlier that day. Something about the tone in her voice didn't feel right. I hoped she and Jar weren't trying to start another pointless war with each other.

Cache's call coming through my cellphone was a needed distraction. It was like my mind always wanted to think the worst. I sat on the phone listening to her talk about how much she was missing Stella. Cache had fallen in love with Dinah's baby, but Noble was adamant in his decision to not let her develop a relationship with her any further. I understood Noble's reasoning, but I also understood how hard it was to walk away from someone you loved. I could only imagine it was harder when the person was an innocent baby. On top of that, she was trying to mend her relationship with her mom. They had decided to attended therapy sessions together. I hoped it helped Cache heal from the hurt her mother caused, and I prayed her mother was genuine in her actions.

After talking to Cache, I decided to drive out to my parents' house. While I was backing out of my driveway, my phone rang. I was surprised to see Aunt Belle calling me.

"Hi Aunt Belle, I was just on my way to see you. I wanted to talk with you before you left," I said.

"Listen Amoy, that boy is no good for you. I just want you to know I love you if anything happens to me. Please don't come here. I will contact you as soon as I can," she said ending the call.

My heart started to race. Doubts about Dachon started to resurface. I didn't want to believe he would hurt me or my family because there was no reason for him to bring harm to us. So many questions started to flood my mind. I called Jar numerous times, but he wasn't answering my calls, and Dachon's phone kept going to voicemail. I sped through traffic trying to get to our family house as quick as possible.

Dachon

I couldn't believe Aunt Belle was the mastermind behind all this. Reginald had to be lying. Amoy's mother and Aunt Belle were sister. She raised them after their parents died. I saw the hurt in her eyes when she looked at me the night she discovered who I was. She couldn't have faked that much grief. Damn, this would devastate Amoy. Maybe Jar and I should've left this shit alone. Now I understood what Juan meant when he said to be prepared for what we'd find out. He knew she was involved after we filled him in on what we knew.

Everything was going through my mind as I drove to Aunt Belle's home. The house was on the outskirts of Atlanta, and I had visited the home with Amoy a couple of times, because she wanted to show me where she was raised. There were only a few houses on the rural road. Their home was so far down the road only two other houses were visible. I didn't see Jar's car in the front of the driveway, but I knew the driveway wrapped around to the back of the house as well. There were no lights on the outside or inside of the house. I slowly drove to the back of the house with the headlights off. My heart started beating fast when I spotted Jar's and Aunt Belle's cars. I slid out of my car and quietly shut the door. I tried looking through a few windows, but the house was pitch black on the inside. I crept around the outside of the house looking for an entrance while still trying to call Jar's phone. I was relieved when the patio door slid open. I reached for my gun, but it wasn't there. *Fuck! I put it in Amoy's safe.*

I took a deep breath and entered the house. I could only see a small amount of light down the long hallway. As I was making my way through the dark house, I tripped and fell over something. I scrambled to get off of whatever it was. When I looked it was a dead body with blood covering its torso. I didn't recognize the face, but I was relieved to know it wasn't Jar. I searched him for a gun, but there was nothing. I moved closer to the room where there was a light on and began to hear voices.

"You killed our parents! You fucking lived in our house and raised us! Why?" Jar asked.

"Your mother wasn't supposed to be in the car. That dope head nigga got so high, he fucked up!" I heard Aunt Belle trying to explain.

"No you fucked up! You killed our father over greed and envy! But you took your only sister's life with his," Jar said.

"This was supposed to be all mine. I brought your father into the game. He came in and took everything from us. He found out about our sex trafficking and cut us off," Aunt Belle explained.

"So fucking what! He took care of you. You never worked a damn day in your life because of him! You fucking killed them and turned around and raised their damn kids! You are fucking evil!" Jar said with rage in his voice.

"I love you," she pleaded. "Your mother was supposed to be here to take care of you, and I would take over for your dad. That was the way it was supposed to go. But it didn't. I'm sorry Jar. I love you and Amoy. I never meant for you to lose both your parents," she explained.

"Then you tried to fucking kill me because you knew we were getting close to the truth?" Jar asked. His voice had become calm. This was when he was the most unpredictable.

"No baby! I wasn't trying to kill you. I was trying to kill that black ass, evil nigga who brought this back into our lives. His father killed my sister," she said trying to justify her actions.

"But you the bitch that fucked that evil black nigga's daddy to set him up. You ain't shit," Jar said to her.

I decided it was time for me to make my presence known and prevent Jar from making a big mistake.

"Jar," I said, stepping into the library.

Jar looked over his shoulder at me but never took his gun off Aunt Belle. She took her gun off Jar and pointed at me. Jar was too fucking calm for me. A man that composed in a situation like this had already decided what he was going to do.

"You brought this mothafucka to my house?" Aunt Belle asked staring at me with her eyes full of hate and disgust.

"Bitch, this ain't yo house," Jar barked at her.

"Jar, give me the gun. Let me or Juan handle this for you. Think about Amoy. This shit will kill her," I said calmly.

"I got this. This mine to handle," he said staring Aunt Belle down.

"You are the reason for all of this!" Aunt Belle screamed with her gun pointed at me

"Jar, don't let her destroy you. Let Juan deal with her. Let's just get out of here. Come on man," I said trying to convince him to give me the gun.

"Put the fucking gun down please," I said looking at her.

"Fuck you!" she screamed as she fired her gun.

I immediately hit the floor hearing three shots go off. I thanked God for her having terrible aim. There was nothing but silence as I slowly stood up. Jar was standing there with the gun in his hand while his arms hung down by his side. I looked around and Aunt Belle was slumped over the desk. I rushed over to help her, but it was too late. Jar was precise with his intentions. She had a hole in the center of her forehead and one in her chest.

"Fuck! Jar, give me the gun and get the fuck out of here." I walked over and slowly removed the gun from his hand.

"She's was fucking evil. One shot for my Pops and the other for my Ma," he said staring down at her lifeless body with no emotion.

I pulled out my phone and dialed Noble's phone number. "I got a bad spill that I need cleaned up ASAP," I told him. I picked up an envelope from the desk that had the address on it. I gave Noble the address and ended the call.

"Jar, you need to get the fuck out of here. I got this. Whose body is in the hallway?" I asked looking down at him.

"Her bodyguard. I guess Reginald warned her. She fucking deserved to die. If I could wake her up and do it again I would," he said with a blank face.

"Aunt Belle, we need to talk," Amoy's voice echoed through the house.

She walked in the room just as I was trying to hide the gun in my hand. Her eyes zoomed in on me standing over her dead aunt. All I heard was a horrific scream coming from her. She ran over to Aunt Belle and hugged her as she called her name over and over trying to get her to wake up. My heart shattered watching her in so much pain.

Next thing I know, she ran up on me and started beating me in my chest. She screamed with tears running down her beautiful face. This was too hard to explain to her right now. I let her take her hurt and anger out on me. She slapped, punched, and clawed at me. She called me every foul name she could think of at that moment. Tears poured down her face as I stood like a statue to be her punching bag. My body was numb to her punches, but my heart was aching, because I knew I had lost her. She didn't stop until she was exhausted to the point she fainted. I caught her in my arms before she collapsed.

"Get her out of here. I'll stay to make sure this is cleaned up. Don't tell her shit, Jar. It's better she thinks I did it than you. You are the only family she has left," I instructed him.

"We'll discuss this later," he said, scooping Amoy in his arms.

I stayed at the house and waited for the cleanup crew.

One Month Later

Cache

Amoy left town the day after Aunt Belle's death, and no one had heard from her in a month. She sent me one text to let me know she was leaving and to give her space and privacy. I had tried calling and texting her phone every day for the past month. I was told Aunt Belle died of a heart attack, but something told me there was more the story.

All the men were being secretive about her death. They would be having a conversation but stopped talking when I walked in the room. Jar gave her a proper funeral but didn't attend it. I was the only close family member there. I wasn't a blood relative of Aunt Belle's, but I always considered her family since Amoy and I became friends. I missed having Amoy here to vent my frustrations. Therapy helped but there was nothing like having my best friend here with me. I was going to respect her privacy and space for as long as I could stand it, but I wished she would come back home.

At least one good thing had happened over the past month. My relationship with my mother was improving. I realized I didn't need her to acknowledge me to her parents. I just needed her to accept responsibility for what she did. Long, tedious sessions had gotten us to a place where we could sit through dinner without me throwing a tantrum. She invited me to attend her mother's birthday party, but I declined. I didn't need their acceptance anymore. My life was full and complete. I had a great man, a baby on the way, and my mother was back in my life.

Even though my life was going well, there was always something going wrong. After finding out Stella wasn't his daughter, Noble immediately started to distance himself. Me, on the other hand, I couldn't do it. I was sneaking behind his back visiting and helping Dinah with Stella. When Noble found out, he was furious. It was causing serious problems between us until he finally agreed to let me help Dinah out sometimes. He didn't have a problem with helping out with Stella. His problem was he felt like Dinah was taking advantage of my love for Stella. Jar even helped Dinah get a good paying nine to five job. When I didn't have plans, I would babysit for her to give her a break.

I was relaxing in Noble's den when my phone started ringing. Taking a deep breath, I answered Dinah's call. Today's answer was going to be no. I wanted to relax and enjoy being fat and pregnant.

"Hello," Dinah said with attitude.

"Hi Dinah," I replied.

"When you coming to get Stella? I need a break," she asked.

"I don't know, Dinah. I'm taking a break myself. I had a hard week of finals," I answered.

"Well he needs to tell his parents to keep her because I'm tired," she demanded.

"Dinah, Stella is not our responsibility. What we do for her is out of the kindness of our hearts. So please don't call here demanding anything from us," I stated calmly before I ended the call. Nova had been teaching me to block out all negative vibes, so I wasn't going to let her ruin my mood or day. I dozed off and was awakened by Noble curling up on the chaise with me.

"Sorry I wasn't planning on coming home this late, but shit got busy. I need to hire a couple more waitresses and another bartender," he said planting soft kisses on my neck while rubbing my belly.

"That's okay," I said groggily, turning to face him.

"You smell like pizza," he said, smiling at me. I laughed because since I had been pregnant pizza and ice cream were the only things I wanted to eat.

"I had some earlier. You look so tired. Go upstairs and take a shower. I'll be up to give you a massage," I told him. He kissed me on my forehead and went upstairs.

An hour later, I was straddled on Noble while he laid on his stomach. I oiled his back and started giving him the massage he needed.

"Damn that feels good," he moaned. I leaned forward and kissed him on the cheek.

"Dinah called today. She wanted me to come get Stella because she needs a break, but I told her I was getting some needed rest myself. I'm started to regret that decision. Maybe we can watch her for a couple of hours," I said. He flipped over so quick I fell over on the bed on my back. I sat up in the bed.

"No the hell we ain't. We just had her last weekend. I love that little girl just as much as you but stop letting Dinah use you. That's what this massage was for? To butter me up so I would agree to keep her?" He asked angrily.

"No, it was not. Stella is no problem; she's the sweetest baby. I don't see what the big deal is about keeping her," I said.

"The big deal is she's not ours, and Dinah needs to be a mama even when she doesn't feel like it. She'll never learn to do that if we're always there to bail her out. It's time to cut all ties with Dinah," he said, getting off the bed.

"That's cold, Noble. What about Stella?" I asked sadly.

"She's not my child, Cache. How is that cold? What we are doing is out of the kindness of our hearts. We don't owe Dinah shit," he stated.

"But Noble, you see how Dinah's mom is. And Dinah has issues her damn self. I just think it's good for Stella to have stable people that care about her in her life." I stressed to him.

"Fuck Cache, there's a lot of kids in situations like that. We can't start taking care of every child that we know in that way," he said, looking at me.

"I know that, but that little girl has touched our hearts. So why can't we make her a part of our life?" I asked.

"Because Dinah is a user," Noble said, putting on a pair of boxers.

"Where are you going?" I asked as he walked away from me.

"Downstairs; I need a fucking smoke," he said, walking out the room.

I flopped back on the bed and exhaled. I knew it was stressful for him to deal with Dinah, but I had become attached to that little girl. I thought about her not having loving and caring people in her life and it made me want better for her. Dinah's only concern was partying and enjoying her freedom, so she didn't want to be a full-time mom. Dinah's mother only wanted something to do with Stella if money was attached. I thought about when my mom left me. If it hadn't been for having a strong father in my life to love and support me, I don't know what would have happened to me. I just wanted to give that beautiful child a fair and balanced chance at life. If that meant tolerating Dinah, I was willing to do that.

I didn't want to add to Noble's stressful day. Nor did I want Dinah causing problems in our relationship, so I went downstairs to apologize. He was sitting at the kitchen table smoking a blunt. I sat across from him.

"You're right. I need to set more boundaries with Dinah," I said.

"We will keep her today and take her back tomorrow. Next weekend is ours, because we going out of town. I'm going to put on some clothes, and we'll go get her," he said, standing up.

I smiled as I stood. "You can't fool me. You wanted to go get her anyway."

"I want us to decide when we want to keep her. Dinah never gives us that chance. She acts as if it's our responsibility," he said.

I walked over to him, tip toed, and kissed him on the lips. "Thank you."

"Yea, whatever," he said smiling down at me.

*****

Noble knocked on Dinah's door, but it was taking Dinah a while to answer. I started to panic, because I could hear Stella crying.

"Something must be wrong. Break the door down," I told Noble.

After a couple more unanswered knocks, Noble was getting ready to bust down the door but the door suddenly opened. A tall, brown skinned guy with a low-cut opened the door. He looked like he had just woken up. Noble pushed him out of the way and I followed behind him.

"Who da fuck are you?" he asked, following us.

Noble quickly turned around and stepped in the guy's face. "Where da fuck is Dinah?"

"Shit, that's what I wanna know too. She supposed to have went to the store and come right back. Bitch been gone over an hour. Store ain't but fifteen minutes away," the guy said.

I walked over and scooped up Stella from the bassinet. Her pamper was soaked and soiled. I lied her back down to changer her diaper.

"We got her. You can leave," Noble to him.

"Shit, that's what's up. Tell that bitch I want my twenty back too," he said, walking out the door.

While we waited on Dinah, I fed Stella a bottle. I held her until she fell asleep. Noble sat across from me on the love seat fuming with anger. Dinah came through the door about thirty minutes later. She looked shocked and scared to see us.

"You need to be careful who da fuck you leave your child with," Noble said, jumping off the sofa.

"You don't wanna be here with her, so why do you care?" she asked angrily.

"I don't wanna be here because I don't want you and she's not my seed. She's your child, Dinah. Start fuckin' acting like it," Noble told her.

"Give me my damn child!" Dinah said angrily, walking over to me. She snatched Stella from my arms.

"Y'all get da fuck out of my shit and go live your perfect little lives. You blame me for trying to trap you when this bitch only got pregnant because she thought I was having your child. You so damn pussy whipped you can't see that. Y'all won't pick and choose when to deal with my daughter," Dinah spewed at him.

"Hold da fuck up, bitch! I've been trying to help your ungrateful ass," I stated angrily.

"You just trying to prove to Noble I'm not worthy of him or being a mom. You won't take my child from me. I don't want you nowhere near me or my baby," she shouted at me.

I wanted to whoop Dinah's ass from one room to the other, but she was holding Stella. I bumped shoulders with her as I pushed past her to get her out of my sight. One more word from her and I'd forget she was holding Stella. I'd miss Stella with all my heart, but it was time to let her go. I thought I could deal with Dinah, but I couldn't.

"You so fuckin' pathetic," Noble said shaking his head at her. She yelled at us as we left her apartment.

Dachon

The night I lost her still replayed in my mind every day. I stayed and waited for the cleanup crew after Jar took her home. Jar and I had paid the coroner on Juan's payroll a quarter of a million to classify Aunt Belle's death as a heart attack on the death certificate. Jar wanted to cremate her body, but I knew that was something Amoy wouldn't want. I knew I was the last person on earth she wanted to hear from, so I didn't try calling or texting her.

Jar was acting as if nothing happened. It was business as usual for him. He pleaded with me to let him tell Amoy what really happened, but I didn't think it would've made a difference to her. I was the one she didn't trust in her family, so she would always feel like I was at fault. She had to be willing to accept me without knowing the truth. I did agree to let him tell her about Aunt Belle. He never got that chance, because she left the city without informing anyone.

"Nigga, if you gon' sit in the club looking like a sick chicken, you might as well take yo ass home," Jar said with a plus-size, cute shawty sitting on his lap.

He tapped her on the ass and told her to get us a bottle of D'Usse from the bar. She kissed him on the lips and walked away.

"I love a close-built bitch. Ain't no air getting between them thighs. Pussy be wet, warm and tight as hell. Juices just sitting there marinating waiting for me to slid inside," he said, watching her walk away. I chuckled.

I leaned forward resting my arms on my knees. "Yo sister been gon' for a month…you killed you aunt. Ain't that shit fuckin' with you?"

"I killed an evil bitch. Amoy will bring her ass home when she's ready. When she does come home, we'll handle things. So explain to me again why we can't tell her I killed that woman," he said.

I shook my head. Ever since he found out about Aunt Belle, he refused to use her name.

"If she can't find justification in me killing Aunt Belle after finding out who she is, shit was never real between us. If she knew you killed her, it would bring a wedge between you and her. She needs you more than she needs me to get through this," I explained.

"Man, that shit don't make no damn sense," Jar said.

"Basically, I will know she loves and trusts me if she can accept what I did. Then she'll know I only have intentions of loving and protecting her. Is that better?" I asked.

He shrugged his shoulders. "Still sound dumb as fuck, but okay."

"Your sister is judgmental as fuck. She already going to give you hell for still fuckin' with me regardless of what Aunt Belle did. It'll be harder for her to accept you killing her than me," I told him.

"Whatever. I know Amoy's every move. I ain't stupid enough to let my sister be off with no protection. You wanna know where she at?" he asked with a devilish smile.

I pondered the question for a few minutes trying to decide if I wanted to know. Something told me Jar knew all along where she was. I knew all I had to do was ask for the information and he would tell me, but she needed space and I understood why. I'd give her as much time as I could before I brought her back myself.

"You think she remembers seeing you there?" I asked him.

"Nah, she still doesn't know I was there. That I know for sure," he said.

"I heard you guys wanted a bottle over here," Lisa said walking over with the bottle of D'Usse in her hand.

"We did, but not from you. Where dat thick bitch at?" Jar asked, standing up. He walked past Lisa without saying a word.

"I guess he's never going to get over the abortion I had," she said, flopping down next to me.

"Guess not," I said, standing up.

I left her sitting at the booth and made my way to my office to get away from the noise. Going home wasn't an option for me, because I would only think about her. I wasn't alone in my office for ten minutes before the door came flying open.

"You better get this bitch before I knock her wig off," Eva said, busting in my office. Lisa walked in behind her.

"Don't you fuckin' knock?" I asked angrily.

"Sorry, but she's getting on my last damn nerve. You are my boss, not her," Eva said.

"I'm just trying to tell her what pictures she should be taking," Lisa said, walking over to my desk.

"Lisa, you manage the club. I manage Eva. Now get da fuck out," I said to both of them. Eva stuck her tongue out at Lisa and walked out.

"I'm sorry. I just saw some great footage she should've been capturing," Lisa said.

"Do your job. Eva knows how to do hers," I said sternly.

"Do you hate me or something? What did I do to push you so far away from me?" She asked sadly. I felt bad for the way I had been treating her. We used to be so close.

"My bad. I'm just dealing with some shit right now." I apologized.

"Let me help you relax," she said, kneeling down in front of me. The offer was tempting; I hadn't had my dick inside a piece of pussy or a mouth since Amoy left.

"I'm good, Lisa. I don't wanna use you for sex, because that's all it'll be. You better than that," I told her.

"I'm a big girl. I can handle it," she said smiling up at me.

My office door came flying open again.

"Damn, does anyone knock around here?" I asked angrily.

"Sorry boss. I was looking for her," one of my bartenders said pointing at Lisa who was still on her knees.

"What is it?" Lisa asked angrily, standing up.

"You got the key to the back room. We need more Hennessy and Watermelon Cîroc," the bartender said smiling at Lisa.

I shook my head and walked over to my desk. Getting involved with Lisa wasn't a good idea. She said she could handle just sex, but I knew she wanted more. Maybe her finding another job would be the best option. It was obvious she still had hope that she and I would get back together. I started to think of places I could use her where she wouldn't be around me as much until my phone rang. I looked at the screen to see it was my old manager, Chantel, calling. I hadn't heard from her since she left to take care of her family.

"What's up, Chantel?" I asked answering the phone.

"Dak, I really need to talk to you in private. Please don't tell anyone about this call. Can we meet somewhere?" she asked. Her voice sounded shook.

"Yea, where you at?" I asked.

"I'm still in Huntsville. I will be in Atlanta next week. I will call you," she said.

"Okay. Everything okay? Do you need anything? How's your family?" I asked. I knew I was rambling, but I was genuinely concerned. I knew she had a family emergency, but I thought she would return to work eventually.

I looked at my phone when a text alert came through. Jar sent a picture of a news article link. I clicked on the link and read the headline.

OWNER OF WILLIAMS' TRUCKING COMPANY AND WIFE BODIES FOUND.

I read the article and learned that their bodies had been dismembered and left in one of the truck trailers. Juan got his revenge.

One Week Later

Amoy

The nightmares still wouldn't let me sleep. Every time I closed my eyes, I could see Dachon standing over Aunt Belle's body. Everything after that moment became a blur. So much hurt, betrayal and anger consumed my heart and mind. I didn't understand how Dachon could do this to me and my family. Aunt Belle hated Dachon, but that was no reason to kill her. Our last phone conversation kept replaying in my head. She warned me of what he was going to do to her. I thought she was overreacting because of her hate for him, but she wasn't. He succeeded in doing what she thought he would do. I didn't remember too much after seeing my aunt's lifeless body. The next thing I remembered I woke up in my bed, and Jarvis was asleep on the sofa in my bedroom. Our heated argument is what caused me to leave.

"Jarvis! Wake up!" I screamed at him.

He jumped up with his eyes stretched open. "What? You okay?"

"He killed her, Jarvis. She told me he was going to do it and he did. I saw him standing over her body," I said.

He pulled me into his arms and held me. I couldn't stop crying. Aunt Belle was like a mother to me. Dachon's father took my parents, and he took my aunt and shattered my heart. I didn't know how I could get over this. I wanted him to feel the pain I was feeling.

"I'm sorry, Amoy," Jarvis said holding me tighter.

"Is he dead? Have you killed him?" I asked. I wasn't asking because I wanted Dachon dead. My questions were because I knew Jarvis wasn't going to let him breathe knowing what he did.

"Nah, I ain't killed him," he said, releasing me.

"Is he in jail?" I asked, stepping away from him.

"Nah Amoy. That shit complicated; I couldn't call Twelve on him. There's a lot of shit you don't know," he told me.

I didn't understand what he was trying to say. If he had Aunt Belle killed because of a street war, I would never forgive him.

"I don't give a fuck what I don't know! He killed our aunt. He has to pay for that!" I screamed at him.

"So you want me to kill him?" he asked nonchalantly.

"No but make him pay!" I demanded.

Jarvis didn't seem upset about Dachon killing Aunt Belle. I didn't know if I wanted to know why he was so calm, but I had to know.

"Aunt Belle is dead. Why aren't you upset about this?" I asked.

He flopped back down on the sofa. "Like I said it's a lot of shit you don't know. I'm not sure if you even want to know. What you seen back at the house ain't what it seems."

"You're taking up for him! Get out! Get out of my got-damn house!" I screamed like a raging lunatic.

I was more furious with him than I was at Dachon. Jarvis was my family. He should've been as heart broken and furious as I was. He stood up and walked to my bedroom door before turning to face me.

"I tried to protect you from this, but you're grown. It's time I started treating you like you are. Aunt Belle ain't shit and deserved what happened to her. When you're ready to discuss it, let me know."

He walked out of the bedroom like he didn't just stick a dagger in my already crushed heart. I fell to my knees weeping like a baby. After shedding all the tears I could, I started throwing clothes into a suitcase. With no destination in mind, I left the city. I didn't want anyone to know my whereabouts, so I avoided taking a plane. For two nights, I stayed in a hotel until I couldn't stand being alone anymore. The nightmares were causing me to lose my mind. I finally powered my phone on and called Nova, and she invited me to come to her parents' house. For the past month, her parents had treated me like family.

"You want some more?" Nova asked as we sat in her she-shed sipping her homemade wine.

I giggled and nodded my head. She popped open another bottle. If Nova wasn't getting me wasted, she was trying to make me laugh. It wasn't a hard job, because Nova was weird in a hysterical way. Some days were not as bad as others, but the pain was still fresh. I knew I couldn't stay gone forever, but I was dreading the thought of going home. Being here made me feel free from what was back home. I knew there was more hurt coming my way when I returned, and I wasn't ready to face it. The guilt from missing Aunt Belle's funeral was hard enough, but I just wanted to say goodbye without hearing people's lies about being there for me.

"I can't believe you actually live in here. I mean you have it beautifully decorated, but your parents have a huge house," I told her.

Nova's parents owned many acres of land because her father was a farmer. They lived in an old, remodeled house that was huge. Her mother had Nova when she was going through the change. I guess that would explain some of Nova's old-fashioned ways when it came to her style of fashion. Nova wore her beautiful, thick hair in a big bushy afro, and seldomly wore makeup.

She shrugged her shoulders. "I like it. Besides I don't want to argue with Ma about my unemployment status. I used the money I had saved up from working to get this she-shed. Dad agreed to let me put it on the property. Ma…not so much."

"So what are your plans?" I asked.

"I don't know. The corporate world isn't for me," she said before taking a sip of her wine.

I laughed. "So why did you go to college?"

She rolled her eyes. "To satisfy Ma. She wants me to be successful. The problem is we have different views on what that means."

"What's your view?" I asked.

"Being free and happy. What about you? What are your plans? You have to face your life eventually," she said smiling.

"I don't know. I'm too scared to even turn on my phone. What if Jarvis killed him? I mean I want him to pay for what he did, but not die," I said.

"Why wouldn't you want him dead for what he did?" she asked. She already knew the answer to her own question. I felt it in my heart, but I didn't want to believe I could still love him. That was the ultimate betrayal to Aunt Belle.

"I don't want to be as evil as him," I replied.

"He's not dead. I saw him the other night at the club?" she confessed.

My eyes grew big. "You went to his club? Why? I can't believe he's still in Atlanta. Jarvis should've at least ran him out of town."

Nova laughed. "I don't think Dak is the kind of man that can be ran anywhere unwillingly. Secondly, I wanted to see if your brother would be interested in me dressed as a city girl."

"Was he?" I asked.

A sad look settled on her face. "My breasts are barely a B-cup. A pretty female with a set of triple Ds was sitting on his lap. I passed their table several times. He never recognized me."

"A city girl?" I asked.

"You know the way you and Cache dress," she said.

I laughed. "We are not city girls. If that's even a real thing."

"But anyway, you need to go home and talk to Jarvis," she said seriously.

"Why? What's wrong?" I asked nervously.

"Nothing that's why you need to find out. He was at the club with Dak like they were the best of friends," she told me.

I became furious. Jarvis had Dachon to murder Aunt Belle. That could be the only explanation for all of this. If Jarvis did this, I would make sure both of them went to prison for killing Aunt Belle. I grabbed my phone and quickly powered it on. My notification alerts started going crazy. When the alerts stopped, I started dialing Jarvis' phone number but stopped. I wanted him to look me in my eyes and tell me what he did. The only messages I chose to acknowledge were from Cache. I sent her a quick message that I was okay and would be home soon. There were no messages from Jarvis or Dachon. I checked my social media sites and saw where some friends had shared the news articles about Aunt Belle and Eric's parents. Aunt Belle's death had been ruled as a heart attack, and Eric's parents were found dead. Something in my heart told me this was all connected. I had no reason to feel that way, but I did.

"I have to go," I said standing up.

"Is everything okay?" Nova asked.

"I don't know. That's what I need to find out," I said, walking out her she-shed. She followed behind me as I made my way inside her parents' house. I was thankful they weren't home, because I didn't feel like talking at this moment. Nova watched as I threw my belongings in a bag. She followed me out to my car.

"Don't jump to conclusions, Amoy. Talk to them to find out what's going on. They both love you very much. I don't think they would do anything to intentional hurt you. And one other thing, Jar knew you were here all this time. He promised me he would let you come home when you were ready," she said. Only Nova could get Jar to agree to leave me in peace.

Miami, Fl

Noble

C ache had been sad for the past week, because Dinah hadn't allowed her to have anything to do with Stella. This was why I didn't want her getting too attached to Stella. I knew Dinah would pull some shit like this when she didn't get her way. Eventually she'd come back around wanting something and would use Stella to get what she wanted from Cache. This was our weekend in Miami to enjoy having time to ourselves. We were on our way to dinner, and I was going to propose to her. I wanted her to be my wife before our baby was born.

On our first evening in Miami, we went bar hopping and ended up at Ador`e Nightclub until three in the morning. We were both exhausted, so we slept in the next day. We lounged around the room until it was time for dinner. She had on a beautiful, crème colored, shimmery, maternity evening dress. We argued about her high heels, because she had been having problems with her feet swelling. She eventually won because this was her night. Once we entered the limo, she was excited about going to some fancy restaurant, but I had other plans. We arrived at a beach. It was winter, but the weather was perfect in Miami for a romantic, moonlight dinner.

"What are we doing here?" she asked, looking out the tinted windows.

"It's a surprise. Just trust me," I said with a wink.

The chauffer opened the door for us. The pier was lit up with candles along both sides of the ledges. At the end of the pier a waiter was standing there beside a romantically decorated table for two. Tears started falling down her eyes as we walked to the end of the pier. After being seated by the waiter, we were served wine.

"One glass for her, and not too much," I informed the waiter.

"When did you do all this? It's beautiful," she asked, wiping a tear from her cheek which were getting adorably chubby from the pregnancy.

"I have my ways. I wanted to make this special for you. I know you been feeling down lately, so I wanted to try and cheer you up," I said.

"I'm sorry, but I miss her. I can't believe Dinah is being this cold. I thought she would eventually call me," she said.

"She will, but don't let her use you like before, Cache. Set some boundaries. I've been keeping eyes on her and Stella and she's doing fine," I informed her.

She looked sad. "I should be glad to hear that, but that means she doesn't need me to help her with Stella anymore."

"No she doesn't, but that doesn't mean we can't keep her sometimes. We'll just give Dinah a little more time to settle into being a mom," I said. She smiled.

We ate a delicious meal that was served by Adrianne Calvo, a very well-known chef in Miami. She loved the food. We sat and talked about our lives together. We reminisced about how much she had grown over the months. She mentioned Amoy and Dachon; I told her this trip was about us and us only. She knew we were all hiding something from her. I didn't want to discuss anything that would ruin this night. After dinner was over, I dismissed the waiter.

"I want you to know how much you mean to me. I never imagined moving to Atlanta and finding someone like you. You tested me in every way possible, but I would go through it all to have your love. You are my world. I want to continue to grow with you through the bad and good times. If we put our love for each other first, I know there's nothing we can't conquer together. So tonight Cache Nashi Armstrong, I'm asking you would you please do me the honor of being my wife forever," I recited to her as I set the open box on the table.

She burst out crying. She jumped from her seat, sat in my lap, and threw her arms around me covering my face with kisses. "Yes! Yes! Yes! I will!"

I laughed as she smothered my face with sloppy kisses. I picked up the box, removed the ring, and slid it on her finger. "I love you."

"I love you so much," she said looking at me. I gently sucked her bottom lip into my mouth.

"Come on I got something to show you," I said, taking her hand.

We exited the pier and walked down the beach until I could see the beautiful, white tent set up for us under the moonlight. The tent was draped with white sheer cloth. Inside the tent was a huge bed with candles and soft music playing. She entered the tent with her mouth gaped with amusement.

I stood behind her and nibbled on her neck and earlobes as I unzipped her dress. Her dress fell to the floor and I kneeled down and slid her panties down. I planted soft kisses all over her voluptuous ass as I lifted each leg to help her step out of her dress. She bent over resting her hands on the bed allowing me to suck and slurp her entire sweet pussy. She was twirling her hips and smearing her sweetness all over my face. I tried to devour every bit of her. I spread her ass cheeks and stroked my tongue up and down her ass.

She squealed, "Fuck baby, that feels so good."

I slipped two fingers inside her drenched pussy as I fucked her ass with my tongue. My mouth covered her drenched pussy and sucked on her swollen clit. She screamed loudly with ecstasy as her pussy drowned my entire face with sweet liquid. She came so hard her sweet juices were running down my neck onto my chest. She collapsed on the bed then rolled over on her back and looked at me with intoxicated eyes. I could only stand there admiring her beauty. She slowly sat up wrapping her hand around my hardened dick. I could feel the veins in my shaft pulsating. She licked her lips and let her mouth drip saliva on the head of my dick as she looked up into my eyes. Her tongue started rotating around my dome. I threw my head back in enjoyment of the sensations she was giving me. She started stroking her tongue all over my shaft.

"Ssssshhhit," I moaned as she started thrusting me in and out of her mouth.

She dipped her head and sucked my nut sack into her mouth. Her tongue was massaging my balls in her wet mouth as she stroked my dick with her hand. I groaned with excitement from the shock waves traveling through me. She placed my entire dick inside her mouth. I could feel it hitting her throat. She would gag and let the saliva soak my dick. I was losing my mind as my dick became harder. Her slurping, smacking and popping mixed with her moans were sending vibrations through my shaft. I could feel myself getting ready to detonate. Tingling feelings spread through my toes making them curl up, and my abs started tightening. I gripped a handful of her hair and she started sliding my rod faster and faster in her mouth. She was loving the way I was fucking her mouth.

"Ggggrrrrrr," I growled as I shot my load into her mouth. She kept stroking and sucking until I was drained dry. I couldn't stand it any longer. I pulled her head from my dick and fell on my back on the bed beside her. My chest elevated up and down as I lay there trying to regulate my breathing. She nestled under me placing her head on my chest.

"This head game a beast ain't it?" she said, looking up at me smiling. I burst into laughter.

"I can't believe you did all this for me," she said, looking down at me.

"You deserve every bit of it and more," I said, leaning up to kiss her full lips.

"What if people start coming by?" she asked looking around.

"They won't. This is a private part of the beach. We can stay until daybreak. We don't want the kids coming out seeing your legs in the air," I told her.

She laughed as she straddled my lap. She started running her soft hands all over my chest; then she leaned down and licked and sucked my neck. When she felt me rising again, her hand slid down and gripped my dick. She stroked until I became fully erect. Placing it at her entrance, she slowly grinded until my entire manhood was caught between her walls. She rode me until we both collapsed from coming together.

The next morning we were back at the hotel before the sun came up. Cache wanted to do some more shopping before we took our flight home, so we hurried to shower and get dressed before we headed back out of our hotel room. Just as we were headed out the lobby of the hotel, my phone rang. I looked at the screen to see my worker, who had been keeping an eye on Dinah and Stella, calling. I quickly answered the call as we entered the limousine.

"Man, Dinah stupid ass in jail," he said.

"What? What da fuck for?" I asked shocked.

"Trafficking. Man, the baby was in the car with her. CPS got her," he said.

"Damn!" I barked.

"What's wrong?" Cache asked as she sat beside me in the back of the limo.

"Find out what you can. I'm on my way home," I said, ending the call.

"Dinah got busted for trafficking. Stella was in the car with her," I informed her.

"Oh my God! Is Stella okay? Where is she?" she asked hysterically.

"She's fine, but CPS got her for now," I said.

"We have to get home. We can't let her go into foster care," Cache said.

"Cache, we have no rights to Stella. We can't just walk in there and get her. You know Dinah ain't fucking with us right now. First thing we are going to do is make sure you eat. You haven't eaten since last night. Our plane doesn't leave for a few hours. Once we get home, I will see what we can do after talking to Dinah," I told her.

We found a nearby restaurant to eat breakfast. I had to force Cache to eat something; she was so worried about Stella she had lost her appetite. While she forced down her food, another call came through from Kareem, my worker.

"Yea," I said answering his call.

"Yo, they letting her mama get the baby. Dinah had a baby bag full of cocaine when they stopped her. No bail for her right now," he said.

"A'ight," I said ending the call.

"Was that about Stella and Dinah?" Cache asked nervously.

"Yea, Dinah ain't got a bail right now. CPS let her mama get Stella," I said. I braced myself, because I knew she was getting ready to flip out.

"Oh hell no! That woman doesn't even love her own child. You know she doesn't give a damn about her grandchild. We gotta go get her," she yelped angrily.

"We can't just go snatch her from her grandmother. Let's just get home first and see what we can do," I told her.

"Okay," she said calmly.

Getting bail shouldn't be a problem for Dinah since she had never been in trouble, but there was no way Penelope was going to allow us to keep Stella until Dinah got out. If it wasn't for Stella, I would let her sit there. Cache would worry herself sick knowing Penelope was the one caring for Stella.

Next Day

Dachon

"**Y**our girlfriend's back," Jar said, walking into my office at the club.

His announcement took me by surprise. I knew she would eventually return, but I thought it would be in some kind of dramatic form…like with the police coming to arrest me for killing her aunt. It made me wonder why she hadn't called the cops to tell what she saw. Maybe she didn't hate me, but I knew she would never forgive me for what she thought I did.

"You talk to her?" I asked, looking up at him.

"Nah, she's at her spot. I think she's back for Pops' benefit tomorrow tonight," Jar said, flopping down on the couch in my office.

Jar was having a charity fundraiser for the youth center he was opening in his old man's name. It was a formal event, and a lot of high-profile people in Atlanta would be attending. I seriously doubted if Amoy would be there. She wouldn't want to take the chance of running into me. If I knew she wanted to attend, I'd make it my business to skip the event. It was something she should be a part of, not me.

I leaned back in my chair. "You think she came back to tell what she saw?"

He laughed. "Hell nah, she would've been done that. I told you she would eventually come home. If she doesn't show up at the event tonight, I'll see her tomorrow."

I nodded my head. "I'm not going to come to the event. I'm the last person she wants to see."

"Man, yo black ass better be there with yo damn check with you. I'm going to tell her everything that happened. The rest will be up to you and her," he said.

"For now just tell her why I did it. Leave the part out about you being the killer," I suggested.

"Da fuck for? I'm done babying her. It's time she knows the truth," he said.

"This ain't about her knowing the truth. This is about seeing if she can love me enough to accept what I did. If she can, ain't shit that can come between us," I said.

He gave me a crooked smile. "You really love her judgmental, spoiled ass, huh?"

I chuckled. "Yea."

Jar stayed and chatted with me for a while before it was time for me to meet Chantel. She was staying at a hotel in the city. I didn't know why Chantel was being so secretive about meeting me. If she wanted her job back, she could have it. I had already made up my mind to let Lisa go. I considered finding her another job working for me, but it was best that we just cut ties. She wanted something I couldn't give her.

*****

When I arrived at the hotel, I called Chantel's phone and told her to meet me in the lobby. The Me-Too movement was getting too many niggas in trouble. I wasn't taking the chance of putting myself in a compromising position. I didn't think Chantel would do something like that, but men had to think about the possibility of shit like that happening.

Chantel joined me about ten minutes later, and we went inside the bar area and took a seat at a table. She was dressed in a pair of jeans, a pullover, and Nike sneakers since the winter weather had kicked in. Chantel was the same age as me but seemed younger. She was sweet and beautiful. I hired her because she was a hard worker and needed the job to take care of her four-year-old son.

"You wanna drink?" I asked.

"Yea, I do," she said smiling at me. I called the bartender over and she ordered vodka and cranberry.

We made small talk about the club and what she was doing back home. She said she opened a small club back home, so she could be close to her family. She still hadn't mentioned the family emergency and why she left.

"What was the emergency that made you leave?" I asked.

She looked around like she was scared to talk. She leaned in close to me. "The fire wasn't an accident. She tried to bribe me into leaving by offering me money to open my own club. I declined, because I knew there was going to be a catch to it. Plus, I loved my job. The next thing I knew, I received a call about the fire. The woman showed up at the hospital while I was visiting my sister and demanded I take the offer for the club. I was so scared for my family; I did what she wanted. She warned me to never tell you or anyone else about the deal."

"Who?" I asked angrily.

"I didn't know her name at the time. Once I saw she was dead I got scared thinking whoever killed her would come after me. I know that sounds crazy, but I was just paranoid," she said in a low voice.

I knew she was talking about Aunt Belle, but I didn't understand why Aunt Belle wanted her to leave. I wasn't stupid enough to tell Chantel anything about the murder, because this could be a setup.

"Whatever her reason for giving you the money doesn't matter now. Her death was a heart attack," I said.

"Yea, that's what I kept telling myself until I seen the man that was with her was found dead too," she said with wide eyes. Now, this was interesting.

"What man?" I asked.

"The man that owns that big trucking company. I saw her with him a couple of days after she offered the money. They were getting in the back of a limousine. I'm scared, Dak. I think she was murdered like him. What if whoever killed them comes after me?" She asked worriedly.

This shit was suspicious as fuck. *Why would they need Chantel to leave town?* Then, it dawned on me.

"You letting them use your club to push drugs?" I asked her. She answered by dropping her head.

"There's a lot of drugs still inside the club. I don't know what to do with it. That's why I'm so scared. I don't know who I'm supposed to be looking out for if they come for the drugs. If I give them to the wrong people, the rightful owner might come looking for them. If I don't have them, then I'm dead. I came to you because I don't know anyone else I could trust with something like this. What should I do?" she asked me.

"First thing we'll do is get the shit out of your club. And I'll see what I can find out about who he was selling for. If this is a setup, Chantel, I will kill you," I warned her. I knew the product was Juan's, but Chantel didn't need to know any of that information.

"I would never do that, Dak. You've been good to me. I have a son to raise, and my sister is trying to recover from her burn wounds," she said with tears in her eyes.

I nodded my head. Chantel was a nervous wreck. She was honestly scared for her life. She was staying for a couple of days to handle some business, so I told her I would send someone to pick up the drugs as soon as she returned home. There was no romantic connection between me and Chantel, but I decided to invite her to the gala event with me as a friend. To be honest, I just wanted her to accompany me in case Amoy showed up. I needed some kind of distraction. If she came, I knew it was going to be awkward seeing her there.

I sent Chantel dress shopping on me while I stayed at the bar. My mind was spinning trying to figure out why Aunt Belle and Reginald chose Chantel for a place to store their drugs. The only thing I could come up with was that Chantel was gullible and naïve. It felt as if someone was watching me, so I looked over my shoulder to see Eric staring at me. If looks could kill, I would be dead right now. He must have known Jar and I had something to do with his parents' deaths. I didn't know why Juan chose to kill Reginald's wife, but it was no concern of mine. When you fuck with the cartel, you put your entire family at risk. I was surprised Eric was still breathing. I wasn't worried about Eric fucking with me, because he wasn't built like that. I walked over and sat across from him at his table.

"Sorry to hear about your parents," I said.

"Mothafucka, I know you had something to do with it. Just like I'm sure you had something to do with Amoy's aunt's death," he said.

"I don't even know your father. Why would I want to kill him?" I asked.

"Don't play that innocent shit with me. I know everything," he said.

I stared him down. "Then you know not to fuck with me."

"You will pay for what you did." He tried warning me. He was giving empty threats. Some niggas had murder in the veins, but Eric wasn't one of them. I gave him a wicked smile as he stood up and walked away from the table.

Amoy

I couldn't wait to see Cache. When I arrived home, she was in Miami. We hadn't spoken since I left town. I knew she was angry and confused about my actions. She opened her front door with a big smile on her face. We gave each other a tight hug and laughed with joy like we hadn't seen each other in years. We settled in her den and started to catch up. She told me everything about her proposal, and I was so excited for her. She was finally getting the love she always wanted. On top of that, she was building a relationship with her mother. At least one of us was getting some happiness.

"I've been so worried about you. Where have you been?" Cache asked.

"Nova was nice enough to let me stay at her parents' house. I didn't want to be alone," I explained.

"You could've told me, Amoy. I'm your best friend," she said. I could hear the hurt in her voice.

"No offense, but you are a woman in love. You share everything with Noble. Plus, I didn't want to put you in a position to lie to him," I explained.

She giggled. "Yea, 'cause I would've told where you was at. What happened, Amoy? Why did you leave so suddenly?"

I was shocked that she didn't know since Jar knew where I was. He was kind enough to respect my need for solitude and privacy. I was positive Noble knew what happened, so I assumed he had filled her in on everything. I replayed that night in my head as I told her everything that happened. My story ended with both of us shedding tears on each other's shoulder. We talked for hours with her telling me about the whispering between Noble, Jarvis and Dachon. I still couldn't believe Jarvis had our aunt killed. My head started to throb thinking about everything.

"Please just change the subject. I will deal with Jarvis when I see him. As far Dachon, I never want to see him again," I said.

"I'm not going to comment on the last statement because your wounds are too fresh," she said, rolling her eyes at me. She knew I still loved him, but I could never be with him again.

We talked about attending the gala tomorrow night. I wasn't planning on going, but since it was for my father, I decided to make an appearance. I would wait until after the event to have a talk with Jarvis. My heart didn't know if it was ready to hear him admit to having our aunt killed over a street war.

Cache filled me in on everything that happened with Dinah. Noble went to visit Dinah as soon as they returned, but she wouldn't allow them to keep Stella until she could get a bond hearing. Penelope was trying to get them to pay her if they wanted to keep Stella. Cache wanted to pay her the money, but Noble wasn't hearing it. I stayed with Cache until Noble called her to say he was on his way home.

*****

"Thanks for meeting me," I said, sitting at the table in the restaurant.

"No problem. I'm glad you called. So much has happened within a month's time. I've been worried about you," he said.

"I had to get away. Losing my aunt so suddenly was too painful. Things have to be just as hard for you. How are you doing?" I asked.

"It doesn't get easier, but I'm learning to push through each day," Eric said.

I called Eric to meet me for dinner, because I wanted to give my condolences. The sadness was in his eyes, but he seemed to be doing okay. He said there had been no leads on his parents' deaths, but he had a suspicion of who may have done it. I had a feeling I already knew, but I didn't know why.

"Who do you think did it?" I asked.

He stared at me. "Your boyfriend. There's a lot you don't know, Amoy. He's dangerous. I don't know how, but I'm sure he's responsible for Aunt Belle's heart attack. Everything he's doing is to take over what our fathers and your aunt built."

I wasn't going to mention that the heart attack was a lie until I spoke with Jarvis.

"I don't understand. What does your father have to do with any of this?" I asked curiously.

"My father and your aunt were in business together. I don't have to tell you what kind of business, because I'm sure you know already. Well, when Jarvis found out Aunt Belle was working with my father, he ordered her to quit. That's the true reason for the feud. She had received several threats from Dak about ending the partnership, but she wasn't going to let them control her. They knew with Aunt Belle partnering with my father, they would take over all of Jarvis' and Noble's territory," he explained.

I was more shocked than hurt at this point. Anger was fueling my heart. I was starting to hate and distrust everyone I loved.

"But what does Dachon have to do with this?" I asked.

"He's like their muscle. He doesn't deal the drugs, but he does the necessary kills for them. And you know Aunt Belle couldn't stand him, so I'm sure he took pleasure in killing her," he said.

"Aunt Belle died of a heart attack," I lied. I didn't know who to believe at this point, so I wasn't going to tell Eric what I knew.

"I know, but I'm sure he caused it some kind of way. Aunt Belle never had heart problems and was in great shape," he said. I didn't reply to him.

Eric and I sat discussing everything that happened. Eric told me how Dachon basically gloated in his face about killing his parents. He wanted me to help set Jarvis up by having him admit to having Aunt Belle killed by Dachon. Jarvis was the only family I had left; Dachon was the only man I would ever love, so agreeing to do what he asked would make me no better than them. I didn't know if I could live with myself if I destroyed them. All I wanted was to know the people I loved would always be there for me, but I didn't know who to trust anymore. I told Eric to give me some time to think about it, but I knew in my heart I could never agree to do such a thing…at least not to Jarvis. I wasn't sure what I wanted to happen to Dachon.

"What are you doing tomorrow night?" I asked.

"Nothing; would you like to have dinner?" he asked. I had no intentions of getting involved with Eric again. I just wanted him to accompany me to the gala, because I didn't want to show up alone; plus, I wanted to piss off Jarvis and Dachon.

"Would you like to attend the gala event with me?" I asked.

"It'll be my pleasure," he said smiling at me.

Later That Night

I was looking at photos of my parents and Aunt Belle when I heard my front door opening. Dachon had a key to my house, but he wouldn't dare show his face. It had to be Jarvis. I was surprised he had the nerve to show up here. I stood up and met him as he walked through the door.

"Give me my damn key!" I demanded angrily. He didn't argue with me. He removed the key from his keychain and placed it on the wall table.

"I have three more, so you can keep that one. We need to talk," he said walking past me. I stomped behind him demanding that he left as he poured himself a drink in the kitchen. I cussed and fussed at him as he sat at my kitchen isle rolling a blunt.

"Shut da fuck up!" He roared at me.

His voice was so loud and full of bass it nearly scared the life out of me. I stood at the end of the kitchen isle trying to hold back my tears. Jarvis seemed so angry.

This was a time when he should've been consoling me, but he wasn't.

"She was our aunt. How could you?" I asked softly.

"Sit down, Amoy," he said calmly, staring at me. I reluctantly took a seat at the end of the isle. He took his time rolling his blunt. After taking a few hits, he finally gave me his attention.

"I'm your brother. Since our parents left this earth, all I wanted to do was protect you from ever feeling that kind of pain again. The universe has a way of reminding us of who is in control. I can't protect you from this. You need to know Aunt Belle wasn't who we thought she was. Before I tell you anything, I need to know if you want to know why she's dead," he said.

"Yes, I want to know," I answered quickly.

"Stay here," he stood up and walked out the kitchen.

I heard my front door close. A few minutes later, he returned to the kitchen, but he wasn't alone. My heart raced as I sat there staring at Dachon. Hurt, anger and sadness flushed through my heart as he stared back at me. I wanted to scream for him to leave, but at the same time, I wanted him to hold me and make me feel better. I opened my mouth to tell him to leave but nothing would come out. Tears started to fill my eyes as we stared at each other. He passed Jarvis a piece of paper and Jarvis placed it in front of me.

"Read it," Jarvis instructed me.

I could see the letter in front of me, but my eyes were still glued on Dachon. I didn't understand why the sight of him didn't make my skin crawl. It made no sense that I still loved him after he killed my aunt. I wasn't supposed to be having these kinds of feelings for him anymore.

"Amoy," Jar said to get my attention.

I finally broke the trance Dachon had on me. I looked down at the letter and back up at Dachon. He nodded his head for me to read the letter. Jarvis took a seat while Dachon remained standing by the kitchen entrance. I unfolded the letter; it was to Dachon from his mother. I started reading and my head started to spin. My heart couldn't take much more and I felt like I was losing my mind. His father intentionally killed my parents. I looked up from the letter with tears running down my face.

"I don't understand," I said glancing at them.

Jarvis told me everything that happened that led them to Aunt Belle's house. To hear that Aunt Belle killed our parents was crushing. I couldn't stop crying, because I loved her like she was my mother. Jarvis walked over and held me as I wailed like a baby.

"You didn't have to kill her. We could've sent her to prison for what she did," I said to Dachon as he stood there.

"He di…" were all the words Jarvis got out before Dachon interrupted him.

"I didn't go there to kill her. My intentions were to keep things from escalating between her and Jar. I only found out who she was when you revealed who Belinda was. That's why I hurried out of here that night. I figured that's where Jarvis was, and I was right. Shit escalated fast. It was her or me," he said. I cried harder, because I understood what he was saying but it was still too much to bear.

"Eric said you did this to take over their business," I told them.

"That nigga lying. Stay da fuck away from him, Amoy. Don't believe shit he saying. I wouldn't lie to you about no shit like this. She killed our parents and is responsible for Dak's father's death," Jar said, stepping away from me.

I looked at Dachon and he was still staring at me. He wanted my forgiveness, but I couldn't forget the image of him standing over Aunt Belle's body. I hated her for what she did, but I couldn't stop loving her for what she did. The same way I couldn't stop loving him when I thought he killed her in cold blood.

"This is too much, Jarvis. Please, I just need some time alone," I said softly.

"Don't leave town again, Amoy. I won't be so nice and give you space. I'll drag your spoiled ass home kicking and screaming." Jarvis warned me.

"Please lock my door on the way out," I said before turning to leave the kitchen. I went to my bedroom and called Cache and Nova. They came over and listened to me pour my heart out about everything.

Next Day

Cache

Noble and I were at the jail for a visit with Dinah. I looked around the small, crowded room as friends and family sat waiting to visit their loved ones. We had been sitting there waiting on Dinah for almost an hour before she finally came and sat across from us. Dinah was a beautiful girl, but today she wasn't. My heart ached for her. Her skin was pale, and her hair was stringy and tangled. There were dark circles around her red eyes. She had a small cut on her lip that looked as if it was healing. I had to fight the tears from escaping my eyes. She gave a half-hearted smile at both of us.

"Thanks for coming," she said.

"How you holding up?" Noble asked her. I could tell she wanted to cry but she fought back the tears and nodded her head.

"Do you need anything?" I asked her.

"Yes I do. Please get my baby away from my mother. She's not fit to raise her. I don't want her there," she said letting a tear slip from her right eye.

"Of course we will," I said immediately.

"No we can't, Dinah. We don't have any legal rights to her. She's already trying to file for guardianship. You can contest it, but Penelope is threatening to snitch about what I do. You know I can't have them snooping around my affairs. The bitch offered to give Stella to me if I paid her a hundred grand," he said in a low, angry voice.

"Just give it to her. It's not like you don't have it," I butted in.

"And when she goes through that money she will come back for more, and if I contest her petition Stella will go into the system," Dinah said sounding defeated.

"What about Shrine?" Noble asked. I had never met Dinah's brother, but I had heard her mention him to Noble a few times.

"He's locked up again and his wife already is trying to raise three kids on her own," she said sadly.

"What kind of time you looking at?" Noble asked her.

She leaned in closer over the table. Her eyes zoomed in on Noble. "I can get immunity if I snitch. If not, I'm looking at ten or more years. My daughter won't know me by that time."

Noble shook his head. Her eyes remained focused on Noble waiting for his opinion. I didn't understand what the issue was. Either sit in here for years or tell them what they wanted to know and be home with your child. Noble finally spoke.

"Dinah, I don't have to tell you. You know the rules to this game. You know the risk of being a snitch. I can't make this decision for you. There's consequences to either decision you make." He educated her.

"I know. I was just thinking with your respect in the streets you could let it be known I'm not to be touched," she suggested to him.

"You know I can't do that. All my credibility would be lost for protecting a snitch. You would be snitching on a crime you were a part of. My name and respect would be gone," he informed her. She closed her eyes and nodded her head in agreement.

"You won't help her?" I asked, looking at him confused.

"We'll discuss this in the car," he said to me.

"He's right, Cache," she said, dropping her head.

"You dealing with a court appointed lawyer. Ten or more years is excessive for a first-time offender. I'll get you the best lawyer I can. Maybe he can get you a good deal. Let me work on seeing what I can do about Stella," he told her. Dinah nodded her head.

"I'm sorry for the way I've treated both of you. My jealousy of what you have together made me do stupid shit. Karma is whooping my ass now. I love my daughter and want her to have a better childhood than I did," she said.

"I promise we will make sure she has a great life until you get out," I told her.

Dinah and Noble discussed her case for a while. She started asking about Stella, but neither of us had seen her since Dinah had been locked up. I missed seeing her cute, chubby face. When it was time to leave, Noble assured

Dinah she wouldn't be touched inside the prison anymore since she had told us about the fight she got into with a couple of girls. Once we got in Noble's car, I unleashed my fury on him.

"How could you be so cruel? I know she has done dirt to you and I understand you're angry with her. But how could you let her sit in prison," I said with anger.

"First, calm down. Second, that's jail not prison. That there is a cake walk compared to where she might be going," he said looking at me. I looked at him with wide eyes.

"And you're okay with that?" I asked.

"No, I'm not. But I can't get involved with this," he said, cranking the car.

"Why the fuck not? She should be home with her child," I yelled.

"Because Dinah knew the rules of this life. When you get caught, you keep your damn mouth shut and do your time. If you snitch, that's your life and possibly your family's if the snitching causes a domino effect," he roared with rage. I was devastated.

"So Stella could be in danger if she tells?" I asked.

"Yes, if she snitch. Whoever drugs she had might start singing and snitch on the supplier. The supplier has a connect. All of this shit is a chain reaction. Dinah is the weakest link in the chain right now. Kill her and there's no case," he educated me. I was speechless. I sat there quietly thinking about Stella as he drove home. I wondered who she would become if she had to be raised by Penelope.

"We can't just let her stay in there," I pleaded with him.

"I'm not going to provide her safety on my name because then that falls on me and my family. I can't do that, Cache. The best thing I can do for you is get her a damn good lawyer," he said glancing at me. I understood what he was saying, but I hated the fact of her being in there. She needed to be home with Stella.

"I just hate seeing her in there," I said calmly.

"We'll do what we can for her, I promise. And I'll see what we can do about getting Stella away from Penelope," he said.

"Thank you," I said smiling.

We were halfway to Noble's house when my phone rang. I answered seeing Stephanie's phone number on the screen.

"Cache, you need to come to the hospital. It's your mom," she said in a broken voice.

"Which hospital?" I asked nervously. She told me to come to Emory.

"What's wrong?" Noble asked frantic.

"Something is wrong with my mom. She's in the hospital," I told him.

*****

I had just started to reconnect with my mom. I didn't want to lose her now. Stephanie didn't tell me how serious the emergency was, but something in her voice scared me. When we arrived at the ER, my mom's family was in the waiting area. I ignored all of them and made my way over to Stephanie.

"What's going on? How's she doing?" I asked concerned.

"We're still waiting. She was at the country club and she collapsed," Stephanie informed me.

"Has she been sick?" I asked.

"I'm not sure. If she had been, I didn't know anything about it," Stephanie answered.

"Come on baby, let's just sit down and wait for an update?" Noble said, taking me by the hand. We all sat down and waited for someone to give us an update. Everyone except Stephanie acted as if I wasn't there. I said I was over needing their acceptance and I was, but it irritated me that they didn't have the decency to acknowledge my presence.

"Caldwell family," the nurse called out as she stood next to the doctor. After my mom left, she started using her maiden name again. We all stood and walked over to the doctor.

"She's resting well. Her heart is very weak. The infection from her disease is weakening her heart, and the medications aren't strong enough to fight them anymore. She needs to have a bone marrow transplant. We have yet to be successful in finding a match. You can go see her but only two at a time. She's very drowsy and weak," the doctor said looking at everyone. Stephanie nudged me forward.

"This is her only child. I'm sure she would want to see her first," she said smiling at the doctor. I could only smile back.

"What kind of disease does she have?" I asked. She never told me she had been diagnosed with any disease.

"Aplastic anemia. Her bone marrow has stopped producing red blood cells," the doctor informed me.

"Can she be cured?" I asked.

"The disease can be controlled if she gets a bone marrow transplant. We've been searching, but unfortunately, we haven't found a match yet. It requires a DNA match of her blood type. I would've suggested that you be tested, but your pregnancy would prevent you from being a donor," he said.

"Does she know I can't give her a transplant because of my pregnancy?" I asked. Suspicion raced through my body. I knew there was a reason she wanted a relationship with me. She thought I could be a match for her.

"No, we never discussed it. I didn't know she had a child," he said.

"Can I see my daughter now?" Catherine, my grandmother, asked.

"You can go in with her daughter," the nurse said smiling at her.

"No, she can go in by her damn self," I said, walking out of the waiting room.

I didn't want to see her. The only reason she reached out to me was to use me. I heard Noble calling my name as I hurried out of the hospital. He grabbed me by my arm to stop me once we were outside. I jerked away and turned to face him.

"Don't even fuckin' suggest I go see her. She only wanted to use me," I said feeling hurt.

"Cache, you don't know that. Just wait and talk with her when she's stronger," he advised.

"I wouldn't give her an ounce of blood," I said with venom.

"Come on, baby. I know you have a lot of resentment for her, but she is still your mother," he said.

"A mother that abandoned me for her racist family. A mother that was obviously trying to use me to save her life!" I ranted.

"You think no one else in the family is a match?" he asked.

"I don't know, and I don't care. Let's go," I said, walking away.

My heart was hurting for her, but my mind was telling me that she was only in my life to use me. I didn't want to give a damn about her life, but I did. My pregnancy ruled me out for being a donor. If I could I would give her what she wanted from me and cut her out of my life once and for all.

Gala Night

Amoy

Eric had called my phone nonstop all day. He was supposed to be my date tonight, but I didn't want to hear his lies or voice. I hadn't spoken to Jar or Dachon since they told me everything that happened. I was still trying to process everything. Regardless of what Aunt Belle did, it broke my heart to know she was dead. I wanted to hate her the same way I wanted to hate Dachon, but I still loved them both. She could've spent the rest of her life in misery instead of death. I understood they couldn't go to the cops about what she did, but I was sick of people I loved dying. Since Eric wasn't going to be my date for tonight, I invited an old friend who I had gone on a couple of dates with a few years ago. We still remained friends after our brief courtship. We ended things because he felt like I wasn't showing much interest in moving the relationship to the next level. I couldn't argue with him, because I did the same thing to all of my relationships until Dachon came along.

I stood in front of my mirror giving myself a once over. My long, black, spaghetti strap, dress contoured my frame perfectly. I had shed a few more pounds, so my body was banging. My weight loss wasn't intentional; stress always caused me to lose weight. My hair was pinned in a neat bun with a few loose, spiral curls hanging. I went inside my walk-in closet to find the perfect pair of shoes. My dress was so long, my shoes would be invisible, but I still wanted the perfect match. As I rummaged through my shoes, I spotted one of Dachon's white tee shirts in the corner on the floor. I remembered always fussing at him about leaving his dirty tee shirts in my closet. I picked it up and held it to my nose. The seductive aroma of his cologne was still on the shirt. Memories of sex with him started to invade my mind. I quickly tossed the shirt in the corner where I saw it and grabbed a pair of shoes.

*****

Marcus and I arrived at the event while it was in full swing. The place was packed. There were so many professional black people at this event; I was proud as I walked into the event with Marcus on my arm. Marcus wasn't exactly what you would call tall, dark and handsome. He was average looking and only stood a few inches taller than me, but his caramel colored skin was smooth and blemish free. The only facial hair he had was a low trimmed mustache. I dated Marcus because he was persistent in his quest, but he eventually realized he was wasting his time. Still, I was glad we were still able to remain friends.

"I know I've told you this already, but you look absolutely beautiful," he said looking at me.

"Thank you," I replied. The only thing that was going through my mind was it doesn't sound as good coming from someone other than Dachon.

We spotted Cache standing in the center of the crowd at the bottom of the steps and made our way down the stairs. I had to maneuver through so many people to get to her, but we finally made it.

"Cache, you look so adorable!" I said in awe of her pregnancy beauty. Her glow was radiant.

"Thank you. I just wish my waist was snatched like yours," she said rubbing her belly. We both laughed.

"You remember Marcus," I said, stepping to the side to introduce him.

"Yes I do. Boy, you still trying?" Cache asked jokingly. We all laughed.

"Nah, just doing a friend a favor," he answered her with a smile.

Cache informed me that Noble was running late, because he had to cover for a couple of workers who called in with the flu. Marcus excused himself to get me a glass of wine. My mouth dropped open as Jar made his way over to us with Nova by his side. Nova looked like a Goddess. There were no words to describe her beauty. Her big, bushy afro was pinned back. The long, black gown accentuated her slender frame. Her makeup with simple but made her look even more beautiful. I looked at her with a smile.

"City Girls?" I asked jokingly.

She giggled. "No, this is your brother's work. I mean he sent me to a boutique and salon."

I couldn't help but look at Jar and smile. He started to blush. "Get that goofy ass grin off your face. I just didn't want to bring some ratchet female to this shit. I figured she'd do."

He walked off leaving Nova standing there with a bruised heart.

"Don't pay him any mind. If he didn't like you, you wouldn't be here," I told her.

"Wanna trade titties? I would love to have a B-cup right now," Cache said trying to make her laugh; it worked.

"No, I'm keeping these. I was an A-cup last year. Maybe in another year, I'll be a C-cup with some dang hips," she said jokingly. We laughed.

"Good to see you and Jar talking to each other," Cache said.

"We haven't talked since he told me everything. I'm just going to try and move past all of this. There's nothing I can do to bring her back," I said sadly.

I looked over my shoulder as I followed Nova's eyes. My heart felt like it stopped, and my breath got caught in my chest as I saw Dachon standing at the top of the stairs. I immediately turned to Cache with a desperate look on my face. She only shrugged her shoulders. I needed a damn drink and fast. I looked around for the waiters carrying the drink trays because Marcus wasn't returning fast enough. Chantel stood by his side with her arm wrapped around his arm.

"Are they a couple?" Nova asked.

"I don't know. Thought she moved away," Cache replied.

I couldn't speak from the lump in my throat. I didn't know if I wanted to cry or scream. Marcus finally returned with my drink, and I snatched it from him and chugged it down.

"Come on. I'm ready to sit down," I said quickly walking away.

We made our way inside the dining hall along with everyone else. I became agitated when I noticed Dachon and his date were seated at the table next to us. I tried to keep my eyes off him, but he looked so damn sexy in his tuxedo. Every time he looked my way, I quickly turned my head. After all the speeches were over and everyone was done eating their eight-hundred-dollar meals, everyone started making their way to the dance hall. Noble had arrived, so Cache went to the lobby to meet him. I needed to use the bathroom, so I went in the opposite direction of the crowd. There was a long line at the restroom, and I didn't feel like waiting. I knew where another restroom was located, so I prayed it was unlocked as I made my way there.

After relieving my bladder and washing my hands, I stood at the mirror reapplying my nude lipstick. My heart plummeted to my knees when the bathroom door open. Dachon didn't see me, because his head was down looking at his phone. When he looked up, he stopped in his tracks. In a rush to get out of the restroom, I dropped my lipstick while trying to put it in my clutch. The tube of lipstick rolled near his feet, and he bent down and scooped it up. I stood frozen as he slowly walked over to me. I closed my eyes and held my breath, because I didn't want to see or smell him. Those things only made me want him. I could feel his presence standing too close to me and I felt like I would faint.

"Breathe Amoy," he commanded in a low sexy voice.

At his command I released the breath I was holding. I couldn't open my eyes, because I didn't know if I would see the man I wanted and loved or the man that murdered Aunt Belle. My body shivered as his hands settled on my hips. I wanted to scream for help, but my body was screaming for him. My eyes closed tighter, and my heart pounded as I felt my dress rising up my legs. His soft lips brushed against my neck making my body quiver. Chills ran through me as his wet tongue licked my neck.

Again, I wanted to say no, but my body wouldn't allow it. His simple touches had my center soaking my thong. His soft licks against my neck turned into soft sucks and bites as my dress came over my thighs and hips. He started nibbling on my earlobe as one of his hands slipped inside my soaked thong. I heard a low grunt come from him as his fingers slid in between my wet lips. I couldn't stop this from happening if I wanted to. My body needed this to happen.

I gasped when he lifted me onto the counter effortlessly. He became insatiable, groaning and grunting as he licked his way down to my breasts. As he removed my breasts from my dress, I tussled with his pants to release his rock-hard dick. His groans became louder when I wrapped my hand around his pulsating shaft. My moans and whimpers were mimicked by my echoes traveling through the restroom as he devoured my breasts. I felt the crown of his dick at my entrance, so I scooted closer to the edge of the counter ready to feel him inside me. His mouth abandoned my breasts.

"Open your eyes," his low raspy voice demanded.

I was too scared of what I might see. He repeated his demand, but more forcefully. My eyes slowly started to open. He stared at me with so much lust and love. My eyes started to water as I felt him sliding inside me. I didn't feel the hurt of what he did to Aunt Belle nor did I feel sad about what I was doing with him at the moment. My body was on a high that healed my heart. I could feel my walls spreading as he went deeper. His lips found me, and our tongues slid inside each other's mouths. He wasn't fucking me. His strokes were slow, sensual, and erotic. My hands held on to his waist as he drilled deeper making my juices leak on the counter. His dome pressed against my weakest spots making me cry out in ecstasy.

He lifted my legs and wrapped them around his waist. Love making was over. He became a wild animal plummeting his dick against my walls. My arms were wrapped around his back as he rammed against my g-spot. He groaned and I moaned as we felt ourselves getting ready to come. My walls gripped his shaft, my toes curled up, and my body stiffened. He didn't let up and never changed his strokes. I bit and sucked on his neck as I exploded releasing my essence on him. He followed me with a loud growl as he came inside me. I held on to him unable to catch my breath.

"I love you," he whispered in my ear. Goose bumps covered my arms as chills ran through me. After a few minutes, I finally found the strength to let him go, but he didn't. His soft dick started to grow inside me. My wet walls welcomed him inside with a snug grip. I gasped when he carried me to a wall, pressing my back against it. I tore his shirt off of him to feel as much of his flesh against mine. Buttons flew everywhere on the floor. My drenched pussy was throbbing and pleading for him to fuck me. My nails clawed and scratched his back as he drilled and hammered his dick inside me. Our sounds of gratifying ecstasy were uncontrollably. My legs were hooked in his arms as he plunged harder and deeper until my creaminess was running down my inner thighs. His body jerked and convulsed as he unloaded inside me again. He stepped back with his semi-hard dick still out of his boxers. The wall was the only thing keeping me from hitting the floor as I leaned against it. I didn't know what to say to him, and I didn't think he knew what to say to me. He walked away and went into one of the stalls. I didn't waste any time hurrying out of the bathroom.

"There you go," Marcus said, walking toward me.

A Couple of Days Later

Dachon

I couldn't keep my eyes off of her in the dining hall at the gala, and I couldn't stop thinking about her after what we shared the other night. She probably thought I followed her into the bathroom, but I didn't. I guess we both had the same idea about not waiting in the long line. I never imagined things would go so far between us, but I couldn't stop myself. The way her body shivered at my touch told me she wanted me too.

"Nigga, is you in or out?" Jar asked impatiently. We were at his place playing poker. I couldn't concentrate on the game for thinking about her. Judging by how quickly she left the bathroom, she probably regretted what happened. I knew she needed time to soak in what had just happened, so I walked into the stall to give her a minute. My plan was to take her home and finish what we started. But she wasn't there when I walked out.

"I'm out," I said, getting up from the table. There was no point in sitting there and giving my money away.

"You been acting strange for a few days. What da fuck wrong with you?" Jar asked.

"I know why," Brandon said. Jar and Brandon's parents were like family. So Jar looked out for Brandon like a big brother. He gave him a stack to sit in on the game. He had won enough to pay Jar back and still had a stack in front of him.

"Why?" Noble asked.

He looked at me and smiled. "You want me to tell them or you wanna do it."

"What da hell you grinning like that for, lil nigga? I ain't got shit to tell them," I said.

He shrugged his shoulders. "I hate that unisex bathroom shit, because women take forever in the bathroom. I decided to make my way to the other bathroom that few people knew about. Unfortunately, the entire bathroom was occupied by only two people. I'll never look at her the same."

"You watched nigga?" I asked angrily.

He laughed. "Hell no! What kind of pervert you think I am. I hauled ass, but I can't help what my eyes saw when I opened the door."

"What you saw?" Jar asked Brandon.

"Him and Amoy doing nasty stuff." He spilled the beans with a big grin.

Jar glared at me. "You fucked my baby sister, nigga?"

"Man shut yo retarded ass up and mind yo business," I told him. Noble and Brandon laughed at Jar's stupid question. He was acting as if he didn't know it had already happened before.

"So y'all good?" He asked with a smile.

I sat back down. "Haven't seen or heard from her since. Don't want to pressure her, so I haven't tried to contact her."

"Don't contact her. Let her come to you. You've been chasing her spoiled ass since day one. Ain't this yo plan anyway? Guess it's working," he said, shrugging his shoulders. I nodded my head and decided to take his advice.

"On another note, what we gon' do with that package we picked up?" Noble asked. He was referring to the product they had hauled out of Chantel's club.

"It's ours. Juan said to keep it for the work we put in on finding out about our parents. We getting ready to take over Georgia and the surrounding states. Juan is our supplier now," Jar informed Noble. Noble's eyes lit up thinking about the money they were getting ready to make. I thought about it too and it had me considering getting back in the game. But I was where I wanted to be in my life. The only thing missing was her.

I answered my phone when I saw Eva's name come up on the screen. The moment I answered she started ranting about Lisa. Those two were bumping heads and it was affecting business. I decided it was time to let Lisa go. Eva was too good at her job to let her go, but I could find another manager. Eva and I fucked around at one point; but once it ended, she handled our business relationship like a professional. Lisa was a different story. Her feelings were too involved.

"I gotta go," I told the fellows, and I stood up from the table.

*****

"What da fuck is it now?" I asked, walking up to Eva as she stood by the bar.

"That bitch telling me I can't sit people in the VIP. I know I'm not the manager, but those people spend big money here. She gon' tell me just because nigga's pay to fuck me after the club doesn't mean it benefits the club," Eva said angrily. Even though what she said was funny, this wasn't the time to laugh.

"Who you wanted to sit?" I asked.

"Those guys," she said, pointing through the crowd. My club had a strict entrance policy and VIP was restricted from those who came to spend a lot of money. I didn't know the niggas Eva wanted to send to VIP, but I could always spot niggas with money.

"A'ight. Give me a few minutes. I'll be back," I said. I took a seat on the bottom floor and nursed a glass of cognac as I observed the niggas for about an hour. They were laid back and observant of their surroundings. I walked back over to Eva.

"Send them up to VIP. Give them my table. Where's Lisa?" I asked.

"Da fuck if I know," she said, walking away. I searched the club but couldn't find Lisa. I went to my office to observe the cameras hoping to spot her. When I walked in my office, Lisa was sitting at my desk on the phone. She quickly hung up.

"I needed to make a call and it was too loud in the club. I'll get out your way," she said, standing up.

"Nah, sit on the other side of the desk," I said, making my way to my chair.

She rolled her eyes as she took a seat. "I guess the brown-noser called you."

I chuckled. "Yea, she did. You are the manager and I let you run this club when I'm not here, so I don't have a problem with you deciding who gets VIP. My problem comes when you make those decisions based on your emotions. You turned those guys down simply because they know Lisa and you don't like her. This has been an ongoing problem for too long. You good at what you do, but you can't do it here anymore."

Her eyes grew wide. "You're firing me?"

"I'll make sure you receive a nice severance package. If you need a recommendation, I'll make sure it's a good one," I said.

She laughed. "You know we started from the ground up. You started making big money and forgot who helped you get there. Nigga, I'm the reason you have all of this. I don't want your severance package or recommendation. Trust me I don't need it."

Lisa stood up and walked to the door. She turned around to face me. "Just remember I tried to love you. You gave me no choice." She walked out of my office. I hated to end our long friendship. I'd give her time to cool off before I reached out to her.

I answered my phone when I saw Chantel's phone number on my screen. She was back in her hometown running her club. I could barely understand what she was saying on the phone. She was hysterical and crying.

"Chantel, you gotta calm down. I can't understand shit you saying," I told her.

"Someone came for the drugs. I thought they were going to kill me and my entire family. I'm sorry, Dak. I had to tell them you had them," she said, crying.

"Do you know who it was?" I asked.

"No, it was too big ass men. They started to rape me in front of my son, but the man stopped them," she said sadly. It had to be Eric. He must've known Reginald and Aunt Belle were holding drugs there.

"Are you okay?" I asked her.

"Yea; just shook up. I don't know if they will come back though," she said worriedly.

"Pack a few things for you and your son to come back to Atlanta. Bring your sister and niece if you have to. I need to find out who it was coming for that product," I told her.

"Thank you. My sister is with her daughter's father. I'm sorry I got you into this, Dak," she said with empathy.

"No need to apologize. I'm glad you did," I told her. After ending the call with her, I called Jar and Noble to tell them what happened. Jar was ready to kill Eric. He made a few calls to locate Eric. Unfortunately Eric was out of the country on vacation, but we would be ready for him when he returned.

A Week Later

Cache

"If I agree to give you the money, can I see her?" I asked Penelope who was on the other end of the phone. She had called saying she needed money to care for Stella. I knew she was only using Stella to get money, but I wanted to see her. If giving her money was what it took, I was willing to do it.

"Hang up the damn phone, Cache!" Noble roared. I quickly ended the call. I never heard him come into the den. I had gotten Penelope's phone number from Dinah when she called a couple days ago. I reached out to her hoping she would let me see Stella, but she hung up in my face.

"You scared me. How long have you been here?" I asked.

"Long enough to hear you agreeing to a bribe to see Stella," he said staring at me. Noble had gotten Dinah a great lawyer and he was hopeful he could get her bail. I was praying he was able to help her.

"I just want to see her," I said sadly. He came and sat next to me.

"I know, and I do too but that's not the way. If we allow her to do it once, she'll keep doing it," he told me.

"How do we know she's being treated right?" I asked.

"I promise you she is. I have eyes on her. Dinah's sister-in-law keeps her sometimes. I'll see if she can set something up for us to see her," he said. I threw my arms around his neck and smothered him with kisses.

"Hopefully Dinah will be out next week. She has a court date. Her lawyer is going to ask for a bail with a required ankle monitor. It's her first offense, so the judge might go for it," he said.

"Thank you for doing this for her," I said.

"I'm not doing this for her. I'm doing this for Stella and us. I may not act like it, but I love that little girl as much as you. I'm just being realistic about the situation," he said.

"I love you," I said smiling at him.

"Whatcha cook?" he asked, standing up.

I laughed. "Nigga, you ain't gon' say it back?"

"What's understand doesn't need to be stated," he said, winking at me.

"Corny ass," I said, laughing.

I followed him to the kitchen and fixed him a plate of barbecue ribs, fried cabbage, and macaroni and cheese. My stepmother acted like being pregnant was a handicapped. She sent over full course meals just about every day. She was spoiling me too much. Eventually, I would have to start cooking meals for my family. Too much of this, and I may never want to cook again.

I sat at my kitchen table as he ate. Noble wanted me to move in with him, but I wanted to wait until we were married. With everything going on, I hadn't had time to start planning our wedding.

"Ma was released today. She's doing better," I said.

"It's about time you talked to her," he said.

"I didn't. Stephanie told me. She called me earlier, but I didn't answer," I admitted.

He stared at me. "Call yo damn mama, Cache. Don't be that cruel."

"Fine I will," I said pouting. Honestly, I did want to know how she was doing, but I was still furious with her for trying to use me for a bone marrow. I probably wouldn't have been angry if she would've just asked me for it instead of pretending she wanted to build a relationship with me.

"If you wanna see Stella, call her now," he demanded.

"You bribing me," I said shocked. He shrugged his shoulders.

I dialed her number and she answered on the first ring. She sounded over excited about me calling her. I asked her questions about her health. She informed me she was doing much better, since they put her on a stronger medication. She never mentioned the bone marrow, so I didn't neither. She invited Noble and I over for dinner tomorrow night. I wanted to decline her invitation, but the call was on speakerphone and Noble heard the invite. He accepted the invite before I could decline.

"How could you go over there and have polite conversation with her knowing what she did to me?" I asked him angrily.

"The same reason you can help take care of Dinah's child and put money on her books; because we are not them. I know she hurt you. You say you have let it go but you haven't, Cache. All I ask is that you make peace within yourself. Not for her but for yourself and us," he said, reaching over touching my thigh.

The Next Night

"Fix your face before you ring the bell," Noble told me. I tried to relax the tense muscles in my face. After ringing the doorbell, I could hear footsteps coming toward the door. I was shocked to see and medium height, average looking white guy answer the door. He stood there with a big smile on his face.

"You must be Cath…I mean Cache," he said, stepping to the side to let us in.

"Yea, who are you?" I asked looking him over from head to toe.

"Cache, I'm so glad you came," Ma said, walking up to us.

"Yea, it's good to see you doing well," I said. If I didn't know she was sick; I would never be able to tell it. She looked healthy.

"I'm doing much better. It's good to see you again, Noble," she said smiling. He nodded his head.

"Here's a bottle of wine to go with the lasagna you said you were cooking," I said. She took the bottle from my hand.

"I would like for you to meet my boyfriend, John. We've been dating for a while now. I didn't want to jinx it, so I kept it to myself," she said.

I didn't know why that infuriated me. She dumped my father to go back to her race to satisfy her rich parents. Noble and John introduced themselves to each other, and we made our way into the dining room for dinner. Noble made small talk with John about sports, I sat quietly at the table, and Mom was in the kitchen finishing dinner. I decided to make myself useful and help her bring the food to the table. I was ready to get this over. Noble blessed the food and we began to eat.

"So John, what are your thoughts on our new president?" I asked, resting my elbows on the table with my hands cupped under my chin.

"Didn't vote for him. I'm a liberal democrat. I was team Bernie. Hopefully, he'll get it this time around," he answered ruining my chance of having a fierce debate.

"I totally agree. How do you feel about racism?" I continued poking for an opportunity.

"Cache please. I don't think that topic is appropriate," my mom interjected nervously.

"No Priscilla, there's nothing wrong with her question. That is the reason that there has been so much racial tension over the years. Everyone is uncomfortable discussing the elephant in the room that is increasingly being fed and growing more and more," he stated, touching Mom's hand. His answer left me speechless.

"Stop trying to throw a tantrum." Noble leaned over and whispered in my ear.

"Mom, are you having any luck on finding a transplant? Was that your reason for going so hard to have a relationship with me?" I asked.

She stared at me with her eyes full of hurt and sadness. "No, I wanted a chance to right my wrongs. Even if I knew you were a match before your pregnancy, I would've never asked you. I don't deserve that type of love from you. I just wanted the chance to earn your love in case I never get a transplant."

Her words cut through my heart. As angry as I was at her for thinking she was trying to use me, I didn't want her to die. I nodded my head and began to eat my food. We made light conversation throughout the rest of dinner.

Noble

We sat in the courtroom waiting to see if Dinah would get bail. The lawyer, Mr. Randolph Barker, I hired for her better be worth every penny. The moment the prosecutor walked into the courtroom and took a seat at her desk, Penelope walked up to the table. She sat on the prosecutor's side, and honestly, I couldn't believe she was even here for the bail hearing. Something told me she was up to some bullshit.

"What is she doing?" Cache asked concerned. Dinah's sister-in-law gave Cache a chance to spend a few hours with Stella a couple of days ago. With her being pregnant, missing Stella, and her mother being sick, she had been on an emotional roller coaster. She was supposed to start her next semester in another week, but I didn't think it was a good idea. She was under enough stress, but of course, Cache wasn't going to agree to take a semester off from school.

"I don't know, but I got a feeling it isn't good," I said staring at Penelope as she conversed with the prosecutor. I didn't know what she was telling the prosecutor, but he seemed very interested in what she had to say. Randolph finally entered the courtroom. He gave me a head nod as he approached his table. A few minutes later, Dinah was escorted into the courtroom in an orange jumpsuit.

"Where's Stella?" She yelped as she tried walking over to Penelope. The guard grabbed her arm to keep her in place. Tears started to fill her eyes. Penelope ignored her and continued to speak with the prosecutor.

"I'll be right back," I told Cache as I stood up. She remained seated as I made my way to the defendant's table.

"Where's Stella?" Dinah asked me worriedly.

"She's with Melissa," I said referring to her sister-in-law.

"What is she doing here?" she asked glancing over at Penelope.

"I don't know. What's her chances of getting this bail?" I asked Randolph. He was a crooked ass, white lawyer, but he was known to get shit done.

"She'll get bail. We just have to see what the terms of the bail will be," he said. A huge sigh of relief came over Dinah's face. I nodded my head and walked back to Cache.

After about fifteen minutes, the judge entered the courtroom. She was a middle aged, black woman so I considered that a plus for Dinah. Cache and I sat quietly listening as the judge spoke. After reading the charges and stating the requirement of bail, she asked if both parties agreed. The prosecutor stood up.

"Upon newly discovered information, we would like to add one more requirement for bail," he said. Everyone stared at him curious about his requirement.

"What is the requirement?" the judge asked.

"We asked that the daughter of Dinah Valdez remain in the care of her grandmother, Penelope Rodriguez.

"What?" Dinah jumped up and screamed angrily.

The judge banged her gavel and Randolph grabbed Dinah's arm to calm her down. The lawyers were ordered to approach the bench. Confused, I looked over at Penelope who bore a satisfied grin. I returned my attention to the front of the courtroom as the lawyers argued quietly in front of the judge. The moment Randolph turned around I knew what the decision was. When Randolph sat down, he whispered in Dinah's ear, and she wept softly. After a few minutes, the judge read her decision which was...Dinah would get bail with a bond and ankle monitor, but Penelope would keep Stella until an investigation by social services was completed. After Dinah was taken back to her cell, I reluctantly paid her bond. If it wasn't for Stella and Cache, I would've let her sit there. It took a couple of hours before she was released.

A Couple of Days Later

I went to Cache's apartment after leaving my lounge to find Cache playing with Stella. Family Court gave Dinah visitation rights until her investigation was over, but Dinah was nowhere in sight. *Her first visit with her daughter and she dumps her off on Cache.*

"Where's Dinah?" I asked, taking Stella from Cache's lap. Stella laughed as I made silly faces at her.

"I asked to keep her, so she could go enjoy herself for a few hours. She's been locked up like an animal. I know she needs to relieve some stress." Cache tried explaining.

I sat down beside her with Stella on my lap. "This has nothing to do with helping Dinah relieve stress. This was your way of getting Stella here."

She shrugged her shoulders. "So what if it is?"

I shook my head. "We've been through this, Cache."

She stood up. "I know! We can't keep her! So let me enjoy her while I can. You don't have to deal with her. I will!"

She took Stella from my lap and marched out of the den. I wasn't in the mood to argue with her, so I let her go. She went to her bedroom while I fired up a blunt. About an hour later, Cache came back into the den without Stella.

"I fed her. She's sleeping in her bassinet," she said.

"What bassinet?" I asked. Stella didn't have one at Cache's place, but she had one at my house.

"I bought a small one," she said nervously.

"You gotta stop this, Cache," I said, looking up at her.

She sat down beside me. "Dinah said if we agree to adopt Stella, she would give up her parental rights."

"What da fuck are you talking about? Are you outta your got-damn mind?" I asked angrily, jumping up from the couch. The relaxed mood the weed had put me in was now gone.

"No; if she doesn't want her, why can't we have her?" she asked defensively.

"She's not a damn baby doll," I said angrily.

"I'm not asking you to let me adopt her. I'm going to do it whether you help me or not," she said with her eyes full of tears.

"Dinah's fuckin' playing you. Where did she get money to go out and relieve stress?" I asked.

"I gave her a few dollars. So what?" she asked.

"And when Penelope finds out that Dinah's letting you keep Stella while she parties, how da fuck do you think that would play out?" I asked angrily. Stella's cry came over a baby monitor that I didn't know was in the den with us.

"You bought a damn baby monitor too?" I asked staring at her.

"Just fuckin' leave! I don't want or need you here!" She screamed at me as she stood up and walked out of the den. I left her apartment at her request.

*****

"Let me go!" Dinah screamed as I pulled her out of the bar by her arm. I had one of my workers to find out where she was. She was sitting with a nigga when I yanked her up from the table. Her screams went unanswered until I had her outside of the bar.

"Take yo ass home to your child," I demanded.

"Cache said she can stay with her for a while," she said.

"Cache is not her damn mama. You are, so act like it. Yo ass could be going to prison for a long got-damn time. Instead of spending your free time with your daughter, you're in a damn bar trying to find some nigga to fuck," I said.

"Not fuck…finesse," she said sarcastically.

I shook my head. "You ain't changed. All those fake ass tears, so you could get yo ass out and do the same shit."

"I just wanted to have a little fun," she said softly.

"Have fun with your child. Ain't shit in that bar or in these streets more important than that," I told her.

She dropped her head and looked up at me. "I love her. I swear I do, Noble, but she deserves a better life than I can give her. You and Cache can give her that. If I don't accept a plea deal, I'll be gone for a long time. She won't even know who I am by the time I get out if Penelope keeps her. At least Cache will bring her to visit me."

"Look Dinah, I can't promise you you're not going to get any time. But I didn't pay all that money for you to spend all of Stella's childhood in prison. You'll get a good deal. If you choose to snitch, I can't help you. I'm sorry but you know that's how it is," I said.

"I'm so scared," she admitted. "Not of doing the time, but of falling deeper in love with Stella, only to be taken away from her. The less memories I take with me inside, the easier it will be to get through it," she tried explaining.

"Let's take this shit one step at a time. Randolph is working on a plea. We'll see what offer he brings back. As far as Penelope keeping Stella, that won't happen," I said.

"I'm sorry for causing all this trouble for you and Cache," she said.

I chuckled. "Cache is trouble for me with or without you, and I wouldn't have her any other way. Now, go get your baby."

Amoy

I could hear everyone's voices around me, but they sounded far away. I sat quietly thinking about Dak as Cache, Nova and Stephanie talked to each other. We were all at my house having dinner and wine. Ever since the night I had with Dachon in that restroom, I felt like my chest wanted to cave in. My body had been restless and every time I closed my eyes images of that night flooded my mind. And then, I remembered why it was so hard to be with him. I tried to rationalize what he did, but my heart ached remembering that night. Finally, I pulled myself from my thoughts to join in on the conversation.

"Oh God. You sound just like Noble. I know she's not a baby doll. I just think she would be better off with us," Cache said.

"Why Cache? What makes you think you would be better for Stella than Dinah? Is it because you have more money to raise her and give her a better life?" Nova asked in her calm, soft voice.

"I didn't say I would be better. All I'm saying is we are the better choice for when Dinah goes to prison," Cache explained.

I decided to chime in. "And when Dinah gets out of prison and wants Stella back. Then what?"

"That's why I suggested she let us adopt her, so that wouldn't happen," Cache said. We all stared at her.

"So, you're using Dinah's vulnerability to steal her child?" Stephanie asked. Her facial expression didn't hold the disgust that was in her voice. I couldn't believe Cache was this desperate to have Stella in her life. Now, she was being manipulative and conniving.

"No, I just don't want her family trying to bribe us or take Stella away if Dinah isn't here. That way we will have legal documents to say Stella is ours," Cache said.

Nova walked over and sat next to Cache on my sofa in the den. She placed her hand on top of Cache's hand and began to speak.

"Stop trying to heal your own wounds through Stella, heal yourself, Cache. If you truly want to help Stella, stop being a crutch for her mother. Helping Dinah better herself is the best thing you can do for Stella. No matter how much love you give her, it would only be a substitute for the love of her mother. You should know that more than anything."

Cached dropped her head. She knew everything Nova said was the truth. I just hoped she admitted it before she loses Noble. The room was quiet, and I don't know why, but I blurted out my secret.

"I had sex with Dachon at the gala!"

The room was still quiet. I looked at each of their faces to see if I could tell what they were thinking; Stephanie looked confused. She didn't know the history of me and Dachon's break up and I wanted to keep it that way. Cache and I told her that Dachon and I broke up because I couldn't learn to trust him. Cache sat with her mouth open and Nova had a smile on her face.

"It's been over a week and you just telling me? I need details," Cache said finally breaking the silence.

"I was confused and embarrassed. It happened it the restroom at the event," I admitted shamefully.

"Oooohh yo freaky ass," Cache said laughing. Stephanie joined in on the laugh at my expense.

"You don't have to be embarrassed for having sex with someone you love," Nova said.

"We were both there with someone else, and let's not forget the reason for our breakup. I'm still trying to deal with that," I said.

"You don't trust him, because he cheated?" Stephanie asked.

"Yea," Cache lied answering the question for me.

"It's okay to love him and move on, Amoy," Nova said.

"I saw him yesterday in the mall with Chantel. I wonder if they were messing around when we were together," I said.

Seeing him with Chantel at the gala event threw me but seeing them again at the mall made me jealous. They were laughing and talking like a picture-perfect couple. I was actually considering calling or texting him until I saw them together a second time.

"Well bitch, don't just sit on yo ass and let her get yo man. Go get him," Cache said smiling at me.

INTENTIONS 2   NONA DAY

*****

I didn't know what I was thinking or doing by coming to his house unannounced. Cache would be the one to talk me into doing something so stupid. A car that I assumed was Chantel's was parked in the yard. There were lights on in the house, so I assumed they were still awake. I had to see for myself that he was over me and had moved on. I parked my car a couple of blocks from his house and walked to it.

When I got to the house, I tiptoed to the side of the house that had a huge window. I wanted to peep inside to see what they were doing. I could see movement in the house but couldn't make out who it was. My heart dropped when I saw Chantel walk past the window in a tank top and boy shorts. Just as I started to walk away something bumped against my foot. The only thing I could think of was a snake on the ground. Forgetting where I was, I ran from the side of the house screaming. It was just my luck Dachon's car was pulling into the driveway as I ran from around the house. He jumped out the car and grabbed me around the waist as I tried to rush past his car.

"What's going on?" Chantel said, walking out of the house.

"That's what I'm trying to figure out," he said to her. I tried to break free, but his arm was wrapped tightly around me.

"Let me go," I demanded. He ignored me, lifted me over his shoulder, and carried me into his house. When he sat me down on the couch, I was too embarrassed to look up at them.

"Why did you make her come here against her will?" Chantel asked him.

"Ain't make her do shit. She was snooping around the house," he told her.

"Why?" she asked.

"That's what I want to know. Where's your car, Amoy?" he asked. I slowly lifted my head and looked up at him. I didn't know if he was mad or happy to see me. The only clear expression on his face was confusion. I mumbled my answer to his question.

"Speak up. I can't fuckin' hear you," he said getting agitated.

I jumped up, because I was the one angry now. *How dare you chastise me in front of her?*

"It's parked a couple of blocks away. Now, just let me leave," I said trying to walk past them. He gently grabbed my arm and stared at me with cold eyes.

"Don't bring yo ass back to my house until you know what you want," he said releasing my arm.

I watched him walk upstairs until he was out of sight. I rolled my eyes at Chantel as I walked toward the front door.

"It's not what you think," she said, following me.

"You don't owe me an explanation. I just wish I had known you were fucking him while you were smiling in my face," I said.

She stepped in my space "I'm not perfect, but a side bitch I'll never be. You are so full of yourself and judgmental you can't see what's right in your face. That man loves you. I'm only here because he's helping me with a personal matter. So, you can go upstairs and discuss whatever you came here for or you can keep pushing him away."

"Why are you here again?" I asked.

She laughed and shook her head. "I'll let Dak tell you if he wants you to know."

"Mama, I'm thirsty," a little voice said. The cutest little boy came walking toward Chantel.

"And before you jump to conclusions. No, he is not Dak's child," she said. I was glad she cleared that up quickly, because that was the first thought on my mind.

"Come on. I'll get you some water and then it's back to bed," she said, walking away. I stood there debating with myself on if I should leave or walk upstairs.

Dachon

When I left Amoy downstairs last night, I thought she had left. She wasn't ready to move on from what happened, because she was still looking for reasons not to trust me. I had to chuckle to myself as I thought about the way she came running from the side of my house. She had to battle with her choice to come upstairs. I was dozing off when I felt her climb into my bed fully dressed. My heart thumped and dick pounded relieved that she wanted to give us a chance. When she pressed her back against my front in the bed, I pulled her into me wrapping my arm around her. I felt her body relax against me. Sex wasn't the goal last night and communication would have to wait. I just needed her to feel safe and know this was where she belonged. I woke up with her still in my arms. My dick was brick hard and all I wanted to do was slide inside her, but I didn't want to ruin this moment. She was probably going to wake up and freak out when she realized where she was. I pulled away from her and laid on my back. It wasn't long before she rolled over to face me.

"I think there's a big snake in your yard," she said seriously.

I laughed. "Should've bit yo ass for being nosey."

"I wasn't being nosey. I thought I saw someone walk around your house, so I was going to check it out." She lied with a serious face.

I laughed harder. "And what was you going to do if it was someone? You ran from a lawn mower."

"What?" I asked. She covered her face shamefully when I told her about the robotic lawn mower. She sat up and rested her back against the headboard.

"I'm sorry. I had no right," she said.

"Not forgiven. What da fuck you was looking for?" I asked, getting out of bed. She dropped her head.

"I wanted to see if you and Chantel were a couple now," she admitted. I shook my head and laughed.

"Get out the bed," I said staring down at her. She looked at me with a bit of uncertainty. I kept my eyes on her until she scooted out the bed. She stood facing me. I tilted her face so she could look me in my eyes.

"Is this what you want?" I asked. She immediately looked away.

"I-I think so," she said in an unsure tone.

"Go home, Amoy," I said, walking away from her.

"I wanna hate you so much. I've tried to hate you, but I can't. I don't know what else to do but love you, but I'm still trying to deal with what happened," she explained.

"Well deal with it, and let me know what you decide," I said with a blank expression.

"Damn it, Dachon! I'm here trying. You gotta fuckin' give me credit for that. I wanna deal with it with you, not alone," she yelped, stomping her feet on the carpeted floor.

I chuckled. "I wanna show you something. Take yo ass home and get dressed. I'll be there in a couple of hours to pick you up."

"Ok," she said smiling up at me.

*****

She sat as still as a board in my passenger's seat. Her face held fear and worry, because I didn't tell her where we were going; I wanted to surprise her.

"You know I could be taking you somewhere to kill you," I said nonchalantly while looking straight ahead as I drove. I almost burst out laughing when she quickly turned to look at me. Her eyes grew big and started to fill with tears. I couldn't hold my laughter any longer. Realizing I was joking, she slapped me on the arm.

"That's not funny," she said pouting.

"I'm sorry. You sitting over there like you riding with a hitchhiker. Relax damn," I told her.

"Why is Chantel and her son staying with you?" she asked.

"We ain't discussing anything about Chantel or anyone else. Today it's about me and you. We'll discuss everything else tomorrow," I told her. She nodded her head.

Before she could discover where I was taking her, I pulled over and put a blindfold over her eyes. She didn't like the idea of being blindfolded, but she eventually gave in. She asked several questions as I drove. She might not totally trust me, but the fact that she was agreeing to let me lead her into an unknown destination was progress.

When we arrived at our destination, I helped her out of the car. Once we were inside, I removed the blindfold.

She looked around for a few seconds before she realized where she was.

"The bed and breakfast? You bought it?" she asked looking around.

I had remodeled the entire bed and breakfast. Each bedroom had a unique theme that provided guests with the feeling of being at home. I had also included a game room to play board games, a library, spa, and beauty salon. The backyard was perfectly manicured with a pier that led to the lake and picnic tables for the guests. Amoy's mouth was gaped as we toured each room. Finally, she stood in the middle of the renovated bar looking around; I could tell she loved it.

"You keep holding your mouth like that I'm going to have to put something in it," I said smiling at her. She rolled her eyes at me.

"Dachon, I love it. What's it called?" she asked still looking around in complete shock.

"I haven't come up with a name yet. I plan to be open in a couple of months. Come on, I got one more room to show you." I said, leading her out of the bar.

We walked up the stairs and entered the room we shared on our first night together. The room was still the same.

"This is our room. I was so damn nervous that night. My heart felt like it was going to burst through my chest," she said, walking into the bedroom. She sat at the foot of the bed just like she did on our first night together.

"Any regrets?" I asked.

She curved her finger motioning for me to come to her. I walked over and stood in front of her. I watched as she unbuttoned my pants pulling them down. I removed my shoes and stepped out of my pants. She wrapped her soft hand around my shaft and started caressing it. Her hand stroked up and down my shaft as her tongue twirled around the head of my dick. She moaned and precum seeped from my head.

"Aaaaahhh," I moaned as she glided her wet mouth up and down my rod. My dick slid farther into her mouth on each stroke. She slurped and gagged as the crown of my dick pushed against her throat. More precum slipped out and disappeared into her mouth. She grabbed the back of my thighs and pushed me farther into her mouth. I could feel her throat relaxing, accepting every inch until my entire dick was in her mouth.

"Fuck!" I groaned, grabbing a handful of my curly hair. I started thrusting my dick in and out of her mouth. "Got-damn! Shit, this feels so fucking good, Amoy!"

My body jolted. "Got-damn! Oooooooooohhh! Shhhhit!"

I unloaded inside her mouth and she drank every drop until I was empty. She smiled up at me as she started removing her clothes. I stood stroking my semi-hard dick as she undressed. I took a step back and told her to stand up and bend over. Walking back over to her, I leaned over and pinched her hard nipples while my other hand slid between her juicy pussy lips. Two fingers slipped inside her drenched pussy. She whimpered and I massaged her breasts and finger fucked her.

"Climb on the bed," I demanded. She positioned herself on all four with the perfect arch and her legs open. Her fat, wet pussy was on display for me.

"That's it, just like that," I muttered. I lifted her ass cheeks spreading them open. My head dipped as I licked and sucked on her pussy and ass. All I could hear was slurping and smacking mixed with her moans and cries of pleasure as my tongue satisfied her. I reached around her with one hand pressing on her swollen clit.

"Ssssshhhhit, I'm coming!" she screamed.

In one quick motion, I had her upper body lying flat on the bed. Her thighs were on my shoulders, and my face was buried in her creamy pussy. Her body was quivering as I licked and sucked relieving her of her creamy essence. I was moaning and growling like she was the tastiest thing I'd ever eaten. Her body jerked from the sensitivity of my tongue against her pussy.

"You're so damn sweet," I murmured. I placed her back down on the bed, rolled her over, and crawled on top of her. My dick was as hard as an iron pipe plunging inside of her. Her pussy stretched open to take every inch of me. Her juices slid between the crack of her ass as I pounded inside of her. Gushy farting noises echoed through the room. I fucked her until she blacked out; then we slept until the sun came up.

A Few Days Later

Amoy

"I'm coming," I said answering my phone.

I was running late as usual. We were all hanging out at Noble's house to watch a football game that I had no interest in. My only concern was alcohol and food. Cache was only allowed one glass of wine and all the food she wanted to eat. What she couldn't drink in alcohol, she made up for by eating.

The past few days had been the happiest I'd had in a while. Dachon and I were getting back to where we once were. He forced me to share my feelings and fears with him verbally instead of always using sex to show him how I felt about him. It had been hard to open myself so freely to him, but he made me feel safe and protected. With no more secrets between us, I totally trusted him with my heart. If I overcame what happened between him and Aunt Belle, there was nothing that could come between us.

"Hey, swing by that lil spot and get me some egg drop soup," Cache said into the phone. I shook my head and laughed.

"Ok, I'll be there in a little bit," I said ending the call.

*****

I was sitting in the waiting area for my takeout order when Eric walked in. I hadn't talked to or seen him since I invited him to the gala. He called me numerous times, but I ignored all his calls. I wanted nothing to do with him after all the lies he told me. He stared at me with a menacing glare as he walked toward me.

"I have nothing to say to you. You told me nothing but lies," I said, standing up. I went to walk past him, but he roughly grabbed my arm.

"You're going to listen to everything I have to say, or your low-life ass boyfriend and brother are going to jail," he said with gritted teeth.

"Wh-what are you talking about?" I asked. "Let me go," I said trying to jerk away from him, but his grip was too tight.

"I have proof they murdered Aunt Belle, and I'm sure they killed my parents. They will pay for what they did or go to prison for life," he said.

"Dachon didn't kill anyone," I said nervously. I didn't know how much Eric knew but the look in his eyes told me he knew a lot.

He gave me a sinister laugh while still holding my arm. "I know he didn't kill Aunt Belle, but he was there when it happened. She didn't have a heart attack. Your brother shot her in cold blood."

My entire body started to shiver as tears filled my eyes. I didn't want to believe what Eric was saying.

"You're lying. Let me go!" I demanded trying to jerk away from him.

"My mother was fucking innocent. She didn't deserve to die," he spat. "Watch your back. Your brother took my parents; it's only right I take something from him." He threatened me. His words pierced through my body.

"Damn pimp, pretty tight grip on a soft young lady ain't it?" A brown skinned tatted guy said walking up to us. Eric's grip loosened enough for me snatch my arm away.

"Order up," the waitress said from behind the counter.

"That's you?"

He walked over and grabbed my order from the counter.

"You good?" he asked staring at Eric as he placed the bag in my hand.

"Yes, thank you," I said, rushing out of the restaurant.

I slumped in my car hyperventilating and crying. There was a tap on my window. I jumped and looked to see that it was the young guy again. I breathed a sigh of relief and rolled the window down.

"You left your purse in there," he said holding up my bag.

"Thank you," I said, wiping my tears.

"You okay to drive?" he asked with concern. I nodded my head yes.

"You don't know me, but I know you through a mutual friend, Cache," he said with a grin.

"Young Thug…I mean Terrence?" I asked with surprise.

He chuckled. "Yea, that's me."

"Nice to meet you. Thank you for what you did back there," I said, reaching out to shake his hand.

"Tell thick'ums I'm still waiting on standby," he said with a smile. I giggled.

"She's engaged and pregnant," I said as I cranked my car.

He laughed. "Damn, should've know that nigga was gon' knock her up. Drive careful."

*****

My mind was racing just as fast as I was driving. So many confusing thoughts were running through my mind. I was breaking the speed limit trying to get to Noble's house. I was scared and furious as I pulled up and jumped out of the car to go inside. I rushed into the house bypassing Cache, Nova, and Stephanie and went to the game room. I threw the bag of Chinese food at Dachon and stared at him. I was sure the egg drop soup had cooled down but didn't care if it burned him.

"What the fuck, Amoy?" he barked, staring at me while standing by the pool table. Jar, Noble, and Brandon were standing there with wide eyes.

"Who killed Aunt Belle and Eric's parents?" I asked angrily. Every one of them dropped their heads.

"Let me explain," Dachon said, walking toward me.

"I'm so tired of this! I'm sick of all the lies! All that bullshit about being truthful, and you're still lying to me!" I yelled at him. I was also talking to Jar but kept my eyes on Dachon. I exited the room rushing toward the front door. I wanted to get as far away from them as possible. Before I could open the door, I was swept off my feet and thrown over Dachon's shoulder.

"Put me down, got-damn it!" I screamed and kicked. He took me upstairs to a spare bedroom and threw me on the bed. I jumped up swinging in an attempt to fight my way out of the room.

"Amoy, calm the fuck down then we will talk," he said, gripping my wrist and staring at me.

"He threatened my life. Let me go," I pleaded as tears started to fall.

"What? Who?" he asked looking at me with fury in his eyes.

"Eric. Tell me the truth!" I demanded. By not doing so they had put my life in danger; Eric could have kidnapped me because I was unaware of how deep the bad blood was between us. "I'm tired of being kept in the dark. I deserve to know," I said as I flopped on the bed.

"What did he tell you?" Dachon asked.

"No, I'm not telling you what he said. I want you to tell me what happened that night," I said angrily.

He took a deep breath and leaned against the wall. I held my breath as he told me what happened to Aunt Belle.

"Jar killed her?" I asked to make sure I understood correctly. The tears wouldn't stop falling. He didn't answer but his eyes told the truth.

"You are a fucking hypocrite. You were mad at me for testing you when it came to Lisa working at the club but what did you do? You put me through hell…made me believe that the man I loved killed someone so dear to me and for what?" I fumed as tears ran down my face. "To see if I was your ride or die? To see if I could forgive the unthinkable. Do you know what that shit did to me mentally? You could have been comforting me as I got over what my brother did, but instead I was on a fucking farm, alone, dealing with this shit. Where was the honesty that you were supposed to always share with me? Where is the man that promised never to intentionally hurt me? You kept all these secrets from me time and time again," I said, standing up. I walked toward the door to leave, but he wrapped his arms around me from behind and whispered in my ear.

"No running this time, Amoy."

I pulled away and turned to face him. "Why? Why did y'all lie to me?"

"The reason I didn't want to tell you had nothing to do with me playing games. You was broken that night. I didn't want to see you hurt anymore. You needed time to heal and you needed Jar more than you needed me. My presence in your life caused her death. It was better you thought I did it than Jar. I guess if I'm guilty of anything it's underestimating your strength to overcome heartbreaks." He tried to explain.

"I would've understood. You never gave me a chance. You never gave me a choice in the matter. And even Jar lied to me," I said.

"I asked him to. You came back to me thinking I did it. You loved me enough to forgive me and move on with me. I knew if we ever stood a chance, you would have to learn to be with me through anything," he confessed.

I stepped back. "So you tested my loyalty like my heart was a game?"

He shrugged his shoulders. "Yea. You judgmental as fuck. I had to know."

I was furious. "Fuck you, Dak!"

I rushed out the room and went to face Jar. My intentions were to cuss Jar out for lying to me, but reality hit me. He killed Aunt Belle to save Dachon's life. I knew he was furious with her for what she did to our parents. I couldn't imagine what was going through his mind when everything was revealed to him. For the first time in a long time, I saw the young boy that he was when our parents died. I walked over to him as he sat at the mini bar on a stool. He stared at me with remorse in his eyes. I wrapped my arms around him and held him tight.

"I'm not sorry I did it, Amoy," he said softly.

"I know," I replied. He returned my hug.

"Bitch, you owe me some egg drop soup," Cache said, standing in the doorway rubbing her big belly.

I giggled and wiped my tears away as I broke our embrace. Dachon walked back into the game room and stared at me.

"Don't ever fuckin' lie to me again," I said staring at him. He simply nodded his head. We all took our seats and I told them everything Eric said to me.

Cache

After Amoy's outburst, our night ended early. Dachon took Amoy back to his house where he had a few of Noble's men securing the house. They didn't want to take any chances on Eric's threat. All the men were in Noble's man cave discussing Eric, and I was on my chaise rubbing my belly looking at reruns of *Monk*. My feet started to swell, and my belly was slowing me up. I only had a couple of months before I was due. When my phone rang, I looked at the screen to see it was John calling. I quickly answered.

"Hi Cache," he said in a solemn voice.

"What's wrong?" I asked getting anxious.

He cleared his throat before speaking. "It's your mother. She's back in the hospital."

My heart dropped. There was something in his voice that told me her condition was getting worse. I jumped up off the chaise and went to the man cave. My relationship with Mama was starting to become strong again. Because I was around her more, I could tell her health was failing, and it broke my heart to know I couldn't help. She had been helping Amoy and Stephanie plan my baby shower for next month. It was supposed to be sooner, but things had been too crazy. I prayed for her to be strong enough until I had my baby. I was actually excited to go shopping with her for the baby and a wedding dress.

"Noble, Mama is in the hospital again," I said, walking into the man cave.

He stood up. "You ready to go?"

I nodded my head. Dachon and Jar told him to go ahead and that they would handle things with Eric. I called Stephanie to see if she knew about Mama being in the hospital. She informed me she knew nothing about it but promised to meet me there.

*****

When we arrived at the hospital, John was the only one there. I was shocked not to see my grandparents. John was sitting in the small waiting area on the fourth floor. He looked tired and worried but stood up to shake Noble's hand. He gave me a warm, comforting hug.

"How is she?" I asked, breaking our embrace.

"I'm waiting for the doctor. She hasn't been feeling well the last couple of days. It got worse this morning. I found her unconscious in the bedroom earlier," he said. I could tell he was scared for her.

"Why didn't you call me?" I asked.

"She told me not to, because she didn't want you stressing during your pregnancy," he said.

My eyes started to fill with tears. Noble wrapped his arm around my shoulders to calm me down. We sat in the waiting area until the doctor finally came out to update us. Her condition was too advance for the stronger medication to fight off the infections. Her red blood cell count was extremely low, and her heart was weakening. She would be staying in the hospital for a while. Before leaving, the doctor told us a nurse would come escort us to her room.

My mother smiled when she saw us walk into her room. She looked so pale and tired, and I could tell by her red eyes she had been crying. I walked over, sat in the chair next to my mother's bed, and placed my hand on top of her hand. She gave me a soft smile.

"I'm so sorry," I said softly. She held my hand and squeezed it as tight as she could.

"Care to walk outside with me for some fresh air?" John asked Noble. Noble walked over and kissed me on the top of my head before exiting the room.

"I didn't want to bother you with my problems. I've brought enough burdens into your life," she said, taking deep breaths every few words.

"Your health isn't a problem, that's your life," I informed her, giving her the cup of water she was reaching for. She was so weak and frail.

"Don't worry about me, Cache. I want you to focus on the bundle of love growing inside you and don't make the mistakes I did," she said with a broken voice as she fought back her tears.

"We're fine," I said, forcing a smile.

"That baby is going to be so blessed to have you as a mother. I know you will never make the mistakes I did with you," she said with a tear sliding down the side of her face.

I couldn't hold my tears any longer. "I wanted to hate you so much, because I still loved you and I still do. Please don't give up. I want you here to see your grandchild and to be a part of all the things we never got a chance to do together."

"I knew I could never make things right if I never truly accepted and took blame for what I did to you and to our family. I'm so sorry, baby. I realize now how meaningless wealth is without love. Thank you so much for loving me more than I deserved," she said barely able to speak. She could barely hold her eyes open.

"I'll always love you, Mama. Get some rest. You need all of your energy to fight this," I told her.

I sat by her bed holding her hand until Noble and John returned to the room. Releasing her hand, I stood up and kissed her on both cheeks. That was the most affection either of us had given each other in years. If I could turn back time, I wouldn't waste a second being mad. I prayed to God for more time.

"Are you ready, baby?" I asked Noble.

"Only if you are," Noble answered with a concerned look on his face. I kissed my mother one more time on her forehead and said goodbye to John promising to return the next day.

Once we were inside the car, I couldn't hold it in any longer. I wailed with my face buried in my hands at the thought of my mother dying. Noble reached over and held me until I was able to control my grief.

When we got back home, Noble ran me a bubble bath. I soaked until all the bubbles were gone. I went downstairs to find egg drop soup and ice cream waiting for me.

I giggled. "Where did you find egg drop soup this time of night?"

"Nova made it," he said smiling. That girl was God sent with her gifts.

I wasted no time grubbing on the soup. It was the best I ever tasted. Noble walked over and sat next to me with a sneaky grin on his face.

"What are you smiling for?" I asked.

"Seems like Penelope had an accident and fell down a few flights of stairs. She has a broken arm and leg. Which means she can't take care of Stella. You'll be happy to know Stella is back in Dinah's custody," he said.

With the ache in my heart for my mother, this was news that definitely made me feel better. Dinah had changed a lot. She was back working and spending as much time with Stella as she possibly could.

"How did she fall?" I asked. Noble just shrugged his shoulders. I was sure he had something to do with it. If she wasn't Dinah's' mother, she'd probably be dead right now.

"The accident happened yesterday. Dinah has had Stella ever since. She wants you to come spend some time with her," he informed me.

"Can we go now?" I asked, jumping up.

"Tomorrow," he said smiling at me.

"I know I said I wanted to wait until after I have the baby to get married, but I've changed my mind. Can we have a small ceremony for just immediate family as soon as possible?" I asked. I wanted the perfect wedding and being pregnant wasn't going to give me that. I wanted to think positive about my mother's condition, but I wanted to live every moment like it was her last. And her attendance at my wedding was a must.

Noble smiled at me. "You know I wanted that anyway."

I called Amoy, Stephanie, and Nova to help me plan my wedding.

Dachon

We could've killed Eric over the last couple of days, but we didn't know what he knew or what he had done with the evidence. Jar had gone back to the family house to check the security footage, and the entire security system had been removed. Whoever did it had the security code to the house, because the locks weren't broken. There was no way Eric was working alone, because he didn't have enough street smarts.

He had called us to set up a meeting which was less than an hour away. I was supposed to be meeting Jar at Noble's house, but I wasn't leaving until I heard from Amoy. She had been gone since that morning and her phone had been going to voicemail for over thirty minutes. The guys I had following her said they lost her because the traffic was so heavy. That was over an hour ago and they hadn't contacted me. If she was harmed, they would die. I rushed to the front door when I heard it open.

"Where da fuck have you been?" I asked louder than I should've. She jumped dropping the bags she was carrying in her hand.

"Jesus, you scared the shit out of me," she said with her hand on her chest as if she was protecting her heart from jumping out.

"I've been blowing your phone up," I said, walking toward her.

"My phone died. I went by Walmart to buy some things I needed," she said, bending down to pick up the bags. I grabbed all the bags and carried them to the kitchen with her following me.

"Don't get an attitude with me. It's my fault your security doesn't know how to drive. I'm sick of them following me everywhere anyway," she said, standing with her hand on her hip.

"Well, get fuckin' used to it. They ain't going no got-damn where," I stated adamantly.

"Maybe I should just kill Eric. Killing folks seems to run in my family anyway," she said sarcastically.

"So we still haven't moved past anything?" I asked, staring at her.

She dropped her head. "I'm just tired of all of this. When is it going to end? How many more people have to die?"

I walked over and lifted her chin. "As many as it takes to end this."

"I'm sorry for losing your men and turning my phone off. I just get tired of seeing them every time I make a move," she said, smiling at me.

She yelped when I picked her up and threw her over my shoulder. I carried her to the bedroom and tickled her until she cried for mercy. This wasn't the way I thought things would ever be between us, but this was the way I wanted thing to be forever.

"I gotta get going," I said, standing up. She sat on side of the bed looking up at me with a smile and started to unbutton my jeans. I could feel my dick started to grow. I knew I would be late, but I couldn't resist her.

*****

"Why da fuck you late? You better not had been fuckin' my sister," Jar said, opening the door.

I laughed. "Shut yo dumb ass up."

"Come on. We ain't got time for a social visit," he said, stepping out of his house.

We hopped in my car and headed over to Reginald's house. Eric had inherited everything from his parents. We had our men following us to surround Reginald's house in case this was a set up. When we got close to the house, Jar and I fell back and let security go ahead of us so they could get in place. Once they were settled in, they called to let us know it was safe to enter the house. I was shocked Eric didn't have the house surrounded with his own security.

The house looked like it was used for filming the old television show *Dallas*. Horses were walking around in the white picket fence. Tall oak trees were planted throughout the perfectly manicured grass. Eric had a butler in a white suit with white gloves to answer the door and lead us to him. I didn't bother to take in the beautifully decorated mansion. The butler opened the door to a humongous study, and Eric was sitting behind the desk with his head buried in his laptop. The butler excused himself, and Jar and I took a seat in front of the oversized desk.

"Your father sure did overcompensate for his shortcomings," Jar said looking around the room. Eric gave him a menacing stare.

"I want the fuckin' drugs you took from the club," he said trying to sound like a confident gangster.

"What drugs?" Jar asked.

Eric jumped up banging his hand on his desk. "Don't fuckin' play with me."

Jar laughed. "Why you trying to act so hard? Nigga, I remember you getting yo ass beat by the nerdiest kid in school. He took yo pinky ring and gave it to his sister. Then she beat you up when you tried to take it back."

I laughed. "We don't have your drugs."

"You're lying. That bitch told me you took them," he said, approaching us.

I shrugged my shoulders. "I didn't say we didn't take them. I said we don't have them."

"You sold my merchandise so it's only right that you pay me for it," he said.

"Man, you 'bout stupid as fuck if you think that's how it works. We ain't paying you shit," Jar said angrily.

He smiled at us, walked over to his desk and picked up his cellphone. "You can come in now."

He sat back down with a mischievous grin spread across his face. Jar and I sat calmly, but we were curious as to who he called into the study. We turned our heads when the door to the study opened. Few things had surprised me lately, but Lisa being here shocked me. I had no idea she even knew Eric.

"What da fuck she doing here?" Jar asked staring at Lisa as she walked over to Eric. She leaned down and kissed him on the lips.

"Would you like to tell them, or should I?" Eric asked her.

"I'll be more than happy to tell them," Lisa said staring at me.

"Well, bitch, talk. We ain't got all day," Jar said.

"Well big mouth, I'll start with you. Your aunt thought I could make you fall in love with me. She was hoping I could convince you to leave the drug game alone and start a family with me. I was going to get paid very well if I could make it happen. But since my plan didn't work there was no way I was having a child by your half-baked ass," she said, rolling her eyes at Jar.

"Bitch yo pussy wasn't good enough to birth my child," he said. I chuckled. This nigga was a fool.

"And for you," she said giving me her attention. "You didn't see my value. I was always there for you, but you couldn't seem to respect that. Aunt Belle thought she could use me to bring a wedge between you and Jar. She didn't factor in Amoy falling in love with you."

"Continue," I said. I didn't know what she wanted me to say. I never meant to hurt her. That was why I had always been straight up with her about my feelings. Now, I wished I would've trampled on her heart.

Making her performance dramatic, she started to walk around the room. "When the plans failed Aunt Belle wanted to part ways, but I didn't want that. So," she said with a shrug, "I started blackmailing her. She had to pay monthly installments, or I would tell you both what she was doing. I didn't know why she wanted you to become enemies and I didn't care. Just like you, I was only trying to make a come up. This is where things get interesting. The night she was killed I was there picking up my installment. I was in the bathroom when I heard the confrontation going on. Amoy's breakdown distracted you.. Your love for her caused you to slip up. You were so concerned with her well-being, you forgot to check the security monitors. As soon as your cleanup crew left, I confiscated everything. You taught me well."

I couldn't lie, my heart dropped, because I knew I had fucked up.

"So, here's the deal," Eric said. "I'm legit; my father was the criminal. Keep the drugs. I'll take three million instead," Eric said with a smile.

"Nigga, that wasn't three million worth of product," I stated angrily.

He smiled. "I know, but I figured your freedom is worth at least that, right?"

They had their fuckin' feet on our necks. That tape would bring us all down.

"And don't even think about killing us. I have numerous copies of the tapes in a safe place. For my protection," Lisa said. She knew killing them was running through my mind.

"How da hell you end up with this nigga?" I asked her.

She shrugged her shoulders. "We both wanted revenge."

"How long do we have to come up with the money?" I asked.

"Nigga, we ain't paying them shit!" Jar barked at me.

"You have two weeks before I turn the tapes in. I do thank you for your time, but I have more pressing matters to attend," Eric said, standing up. He walked out of the room with Lisa on his arm.

"Let's get da fuck outta here," I said, standing up.

Neither of us spoke until we got in my car.

"Who we killing first?" Jar asked seriously.

I chuckled. "We ain't killing nobody. Not yet that is. Greed is going to be the death of one of them. You play Eric and I'll play Lisa."

"Oh shit. Convince each of them to get rid of the other to have all the money to their selves," Jar said.

"Yea; we keeping our hands clean on this one," I said.

One Week Later

Cache

My wedding day had finally come, and I was so happy that my girls had made it happen in a week. Our wedding was being held in a room at the country club. There were only about thirty people in attendance for our special day. I never thought I would find a man to love me like Noble did. But I realized I needed more than his love to be happy. I needed to heal from the hurt that was in my heart. Forgiving my mother and accepting her love helped to bring so much more joy in my life. My only regret was wasting so many years being mad at her.

As I stared at myself in the mirror, I became emotional. I wore a pale pink, full length A-line, sleeveless dress with a V-neck. My eyes teared up as I rubbed my hand over my belly admiring myself in the mirror.

"Don't cry, you'll ruin your make up," Amoy said smiling at me. I fanned my face with my hands to dry the tears that filled my eyes. There was a knock at the door, and Amoy walked over and slightly opened the door.

"Come in, she's ready," Amoy said, opening the door wider.

My father stopped in his tracks and I could see him start to tear him. "You are stunning."

"Thanks Daddy," I said, walking toward him. We embraced each other for a long time. He was always there for me. He was my rock through all my hard times.

"You are beautiful, Cache," Charlotte, my stepmother, said. I released him and gave her a hug.

"Where's knucklehead?" I asked about my baby brother.

"Jar assigned him to help sit the few guests that are attending," Daddy answered.

"I'm going to step out. Text me when you're ready," Amoy said, raising her phone.

"Ok," I said, nodding my head.

"I'm going to take Charlotte to her seat. I'll be waiting to walk you down the aisle," Daddy said, winking at me.

I gave him another tight hug. "I love you, Daddy."

Just as I was getting ready to text Amoy, there was another knock on the door. I opened the door to see John standing behind my mother who was sitting in a wheelchair. She didn't look her best, but she looked beautiful to me. Stephanie did a great job beating her face and styling her hair.

"I was wondering if you were going to make it," I said smiling at her.

"I would never miss this day," she said, reaching for my hand.

John wheeled Mama into the dressing room and stood out in the hallway. I sat down on the love seat to be eye level with her.

"You look so beautiful, Cache," she said tearing up.

I smiled. "Please don't cry, because then I'm going to cry and ruin my makeup."

She giggled. "Ok, I won't. You have a fantastic guy, Cache. He truly loves you, and I can see how much he means to you. I'm so happy for you. I have made peace with my wrongs. I just pray my family does the same one day; if not, they don't deserve the kind of love you have to offer."

I gently wrapped my arms around her. "Thank you, Mama. I love you."

"Oh God, I've waited so long to hear those words from you. I love you so much, baby," she said softly, returning my embrace. Her frail body was so weak, I could barely feel her arms around me.

John knocked on the door and peeped inside.

"I think Noble is starting to wonder if you're having second thoughts," he said smiling.

Mama and I laughed. "Tell Amoy I'm ready."

It was my day to walk down the aisle to become Mrs. Noble Stiles. Amoy, Nova, and Stephanie were walking down the aisle with Dachon, Jar, and Noble's baby brother Mike. I looked ahead and spotted Noble looking sexy and handsome in his white tux. He smiled as our eyes met. The music started playing and Nova started singing. *I Promise* by CeCe Winans. We stood there staring at each other knowing this was forever, for our family, for the love we shared.

When it was Noble's turn to read his vows, I couldn't stop the waterworks. This man truly loved me, and all I did was give him a hard time. My goal in this marriage was to help complete our family with love, support, and understanding.

After the wedding, Amoy made the announcement for everyone to join us for the reception in the reception hall. As everyone exited the room, I hugged and chatted with everyone that was gracious enough to bless us with their presence.

Dinah allowed Mrs. Margaret to bring Stella to our wedding. She looked so adorable in her little pink lace dress. The reception was filled with love; we forgot about all the craziness that had been our lives as dancing and laughter filled the reception room. As I danced with my new husband, I looked over at Amoy. She looked so happy slow dancing with Dachon.

"We gotta get going. Our flight leaves in a few. We need to make a pit stop before we leave," Noble whispered in my ear. I couldn't wait to enjoy our honeymoon in Bora Bora.

We made our rounds thanking and hugging everyone for sharing this day with us. Everyone threw rice at us as we left the country club.

*****

We turned the opposite direction that took us away from the city.

"Where are we going?" I asked curiously.

"It's a surprise," he said smiling at me.

The limo rode until we pulled into a long driveway that led to a beautiful mini mansion. I looked at Noble with wide eyes.

"Welcome home, baby," he said, kissing the back of my hand. I burst into tears.

Once we arrived in front of the house, he helped me out of the limo.

"It hasn't been furnished yet; I wanted to let you do that," he said, walking me up the stairs. I was speechless as my mouth dropped in shock.

"When?" I asked.

"The moment you accepted my proposal. Once I approved the design, I signed all the paperwork," he informed me.

"Who designed this? It's beautiful," I asked looking at the unique architectural work on the outside.

"Nigga that goes by the name Bull," he said.

We made our way inside the house. It was a two-story, white, stone brick home with eight bedrooms, five full bathrooms and three half bathrooms. There was a four-car garage. The kitchen was huge with spacious counter space and a gigantic dining room. We had a theatre room and study room. Our master bedroom was on the second floor, and it had two huge walk-in closets. The windows were tall and pushed open from the middle. The bathroom had dual counter sinks, a huge basin tube and separate enormous walk in showers. I was completely blown away by the immaculate home he purchased for us.

"You like it?" he asked.

"Oh my God, Noble; I love it!" I screamed. I started showering his face with kisses.

"Soon as you finish decorating, we can move in," he let me know.

I walked to the back and there was a built-in giant pool and plenty of yard for our little ones to run and play. I was going to give this man however many kids he wanted. This was truly like a dream come true.

"You have no idea of the things I would do to you if this place had a bed," I said, hugging his neck. He laughed hugging me tight.

"We'll have plenty of time for that on our honeymoon," he said, squeezing my ass cheeks.

Three Days Later

Dachon

"**A**re you going to tell me what's going on or keep me in the dark as usual?" Amoy asked, standing in the doorway of my bedroom with her hand on her hip.

I debated if I should tell her about me and Jar's plan; then I remembered my promise to never lie or keep anything from her again. She walked in and sat down on the side of the bed and listened to what Eric and Lisa wanted from Jar and me.

"Dat bitch!" she yelped.

"Who? Lisa or Eric?" I asked.

"Well I can understand why Eric is mad, but Lisa is mad because you don't love her, and Jar didn't love her. So, what's the plan?" she asked.

"You won't like it, so I'd rather not tell you," I said.

"Tell me anyway. Better I be mad now than later," she said.

"We're playing them against each other. Instead of the three million, we offered five million to kill the other," I told her.

She stared at me for a few seconds. It was as if she was trying to see if I was serious about the plan.

"Either of them took the bait?" she asked nonchalantly. Her attitude shocked me.

"You cool with this?" I asked.

"I'm sick of people trying to hurt the people I love. If that's what it takes to end all of this…so be it," she said.

"So you thuggin' now?" I asked, smiling at her.

"No, I'm just choosing to do and accept what it takes to keep the people I love in my life. It still saddens me about Aunt Belle, but she had to reap her deeds. I just hate it had to be by Jar's hand, but I guess that's karma for what she did," she said.

I kneeled down in front of her. "I love you and will die protecting you and what we have together."

She stared at me. "If you die on me, I'll never forgive you."

I laughed, but knowing her, she probably wouldn't. The thought of sliding my dick inside of her crossed my mind until my phone rang. I quickly answered when I saw Jar's number.

"Eric wants to meet with us right now," he said.

"On my way," I said ending the call.

"What's going on?" she asked.

"I think Eric is going to take the deal," I said.

"I'm shocked. Eric has inherited everything from his parents, so he doesn't need that money. I thought it would be Lisa, because she's the desperate one," she said.

"Greed is a mothafucka," I said, standing up.

"Please be careful," she said. I kissed her softly on the lips and asked her if she had any plans. She told me she was going to dinner with Nova.

"Don't be trying to lose the men trailing you Amoy," I warned her.

She laughed. "I won't. I promise."

*****

We weren't stupid enough to meet Eric at his house. He could have the place wired to entrap us with conspiracy to commit murder on top of Aunt Belle's death. While we were sitting in my office at the club waiting on Eric, Lisa called my phone. She wanted to discuss the plan to kill Eric, so we made plans to meet later tonight. Jar had taken care of things on his end, so we just needed one of them to make the stupid decision to kill the other one.

Eric walked into my office with two bodyguards. He was comical, because he was trying to act hard. He had never been about the street life and never would be, but he might get his wish to learn a few things about our life if the plan worked the way we wanted it to play out. Jar checked Eric to make sure he wasn't wearing a wire. The two bodyguards left the room for us to talk business.

"If I agree to this; I want two million upfront," he said, taking a seat.

"We can make that happen, but we have conditions. We make the decision on how you will end her life," I said.

"I'm not into that torturing shit," Eric said.

Jar laughed. "Nigga, you ain't into criminal activity but here you are planning to kill someone you fucking for money. Just blow her fuckin' brains out."

"Where's Lisa keeping the copies?" I asked.

"Once I get my five million, I will tell you," he said.

Jar and I laughed.

"Nah, we give you the two mil, you kill Lisa and tell us where the copies are. Then you get the rest of your money," Jar said.

Eric sat there in deep thought. I could tell he was second guessing his decision. I started to get nervous thinking he might back out of the plan.

"Do you know why I brought this offer to you?" I asked him.

"Because you have a heart?" he asked sarcastically.

I chuckled. "Because Lisa propositioned me with this very offer. She said she would kill you and give up all the copies of the tape if we paid her five million. We brought the offer to you, because you have more of a reason to want revenge. Your mother, my father, and Jar's parents were a causality of war that your father and Aunt

Belle caused. They brought this entire mess to our doorsteps. It's time to bring it to an end."

"I don't need your sympathy. I want my five million. You will pay for killing my parents," Eric said.

I simply nodded my head. If he thought he was about this life, I was going to let him live it for the rest of his life.

"I choose the place. I don't trust either of you…thugs," he said.

"That's fine with us. We don't even have to know the time. Just let us know when it's done, so we can see her dead body. That's the only way you'll get the rest of the money," Jar said. "And before you even think about taking the two million and leaving, it would be wise to think of your dear sweet grandmother," Jar said with a smile.

"Mothafucka!" Eric jumped up from his seat and lunged at Jar. Eric landed on his back from Jar's blow to the face.

"Nigga, you think we gon' give you two million dollars and take your word? Somebody's watching her every move right now. He has a thing for sweet little old ladies. I would hate to see your Granny suffer because of your poor choices," I said.

Eric stood up. "Have my money to me by six o'clock tomorrow evening."

"Just curious. What are you planning to do with the money?" Jar asked.

"Sell the business and get the fuck away from here. That money will give me a comfortable life," he said before walking out of the office.

"You think he'll go through with it?" I asked Jar a few moments after Eric left.

"If he doesn't, I'm killing his granny. If I spend the rest of my life in prison, he'll spend the rest of his life knowing he caused his grandma's death. Niggas love their grannies," Jar said.

I laughed. "Not me."

"Sorry man. You wanna hug?" he asked jokingly.

I laughed. "Fuck you."

Amoy

"I can't believe you're leaving. I'm going to miss you," I said to Nova as we sat in the restaurant. She had decided to give the corporate world another try, so she was moving to Alabama for a job offer.

"I'll miss you too, but I'll be coming home to visit. Huntsville isn't far from here," she said.

"You told Jarvis?" I asked. I didn't know what kind of relationship they had. One minute they seemed like a couple, the next their friendship was platonic.

She looked sad. "Jar doesn't see me that way. I'm not his type. He likes fast girls. I'm too boring."

"Have you ever told him how you feel?" I asked.

"Of course not. It's strange, because I can feel the energy between us. And at times it seems he can too, but then he pulls away," she said.

"Maybe time away from you will make him miss you and realize how much he likes you," I said smiling at her.

She giggled. "I doubt it."

I spotted Lisa walk into the restaurant; she took a seat at the bar. I tried not to let the sight of her ruin my evening, but every time I looked in her direction, I became angrier.

"I'll be back," I said to Nova.

I walked over to the bar and stood behind her. She looked through the bar's mirror and spun around on the stool to face me with a wicked smile on her face.

"Can I speak to you in private?" I asked.

"Sure," she said, standing up.

She followed me into the restroom and leaned against the wall with her hands folded over her chest. I waited until a couple of ladies exited the restroom before I spoke.

"Why are you doing this, Lisa?" I asked.

"Doing what?" she asked.

"Don't play dumb with me. Dachon told me about the blackmail. I can't believe you knew how evil Aunt Belle was and didn't tell us. We've never done anything to you," I said.

"No you haven't. But I've done everything for Dak only for him to turn his back on me for you. If I can't have him, I'll take his money," she stated.

"All this because he doesn't want you?" I asked.

"Bitch please. He may not love me but trust me, he's been fucking the shit out of me trying to convince me to give him the tapes. The dicks not worth three million though," she said smiling.

Anger fueled me. I rushed toward her and grabbed a handful of her weave. My fist rammed into her mouth causing blood to splatter. I released her hair and she stumbled backwards. She let out a loud scream and charged me, knocking me to the floor. We tussled on the floor trying to get leverage over the other one while punching, scratching and rolling around. She rolled on top of me and slammed her fist into the side of my face. The jab was so hard the side of my face started to throb, but that infuriated me. I used all the strength I had to flip her over. She clawed her nails into my skin as I straddled her. My fists started pounding into her face with no mercy until she started screaming for help. I stood up and kicked her repeatedly with my Fendi boots. She was pleading for me to stop, but I couldn't. She was like a punching bag for me to release all the anger and hurt that I had been holding inside. Grabbing a handful of her weave, I drug her to one of the stalls and stuck her head in the toilet. All of a sudden, I was yanked away from her. One of my security guys threw me over his shoulder and carried me out of the club.

*****

I knew Dachon was furious with me, because he wasn't answering any of my calls. When I entered his house, it was dark. I knew he was home because his car was parked in the driveway. I made my way upstairs to find him lying in the bed watching television. The television was the only thing giving light in the dark room. He never bothered to look at me. His eyes stayed on the sports channel he was watching. I went to the bathroom to check the bruises on my face. I had a small cut on my lip, a bruise under my eye, and my hair was a mess. I took a long, hot shower and wrapped a towel around my wet body. I walked over and stood on his side of the bed.

"Are you going to talk to me?" I asked. He ignored me, so I climbed on the bed and straddled his lap.

"Get up," he said never looking at me.

"She said you've been fucking her," I said.

He finally looked at me with a menacing stare. "And you believed her?"

"No, but she made me mad when she said yo dick wasn't worth three million dollars. There's only so many lies I can take," I said smiling at him.

I tried to keep a straight face but started laughing. "Fighting in the damn restaurant like some ratchet ass female. Leave this shit to us, Amoy. We got this."

"I know, but I thought maybe I could reason with her," I said.

"Well, we see how that turned out," he said shaking his head.

"Baby, that bitch cock strong but she met her match tonight," I said, throwing punches in the air like I was fighting.

"Yo corny ass," he said laughing.

"Got me all worked up," I said.

I removed my towel and he bit down on his bottom lip. Lifting my body from his lap, I reached down and pulled his hard dick from his boxers.

"You better not fall off," he said with a serious face.

I slowly slid down and felt his crown open my wet tunnel. Tightening my walls, I sucked him inside me. My hands massaged my breasts as his strong hands massaged my thighs. My ass cheeks bounced and jiggled as I bounced up and down on his dick. My juices spilled from me and onto his shaft. He sat up, while still buried deep inside me, and started licking and sucking my breasts. My hips started winding making his crown hit all my sensitive spots. My moans became louder as he bit and tugged on my hard nipples. His fingers dug into my ass cheeks and spread them apart. I threw my head back and cried out to God as his dick rammed against my g-spot. My entire body shivered, and I saturated his dick with my cream.

"Don't fuckin' quit on me," he demanded roughly.

He grabbed me by my waist and started bouncing me up and down on his dick. Slapping and gushing wet sounds echoed through the bedroom. My breasts bounced up and down, and my ass jiggled uncontrollably. My slippery walls were gripping him so tight I could feel the veins running through his shaft.

"Fuck! This pussy good!" He barked, smacking me on the ass.

I pressed my hands against his chest and pushed him back on the bed. Lifting up just enough to turn my body around, I started to ride his dick backwards. He started slapping my ass cheeks as I twerked on his dick. He grabbed my ankles causing my torso to lay flat between his legs.

"Keep pounding that pussy on this dick," he groaned.

Chilling sensations ran through my body as he licked and sucked on my toes. Another orgasm tore through my body. After he satisfied each of my toes, he grabbed me by my thighs yanking me off his dick and sitting my cream covered pussy on his face. His licking, slurping and sucking sounds made my hips twirl. His tongue slipped between my ass cheeks and gave my ass the same attention as my pussy. I leaned forward and covered his dick with my wet mouth. His groans sent vibrations through my pussy and ass as I swallowed him whole. The more he ate me out, the harder I sucked on him. My hand massaged his cum filled balls while my mouth continued to bring him to the edge. He finally lost concentration and laid back to let me finish him off. The more he groaned, the harder and faster I bobbed my head until his body locked up and started convulsing.

"Aaaarrrgghhh! Fuuuuccckk!" he roared as he released inside my mouth. I let his sweet thick milk glide down my throat until he was empty. His body continued to jerk as I climbed off of him. We lay there trying to catch our breath. It wasn't long before I heard his loud snores. I giggled and thought...*I whooped two asses today.*

Dachon

 igga, you eating salmon? That shit stank," I said, frowning up at Jar.

"Yea, these mugs good as hell. Gotta eat 'em with the grits and pork and beans. Don't use baked beans, gotta be the Van Camp's Pork and Beans," he said.

"You telling me like I'm going to try that shit," I said.

"Nigga, you from South Georgia. Don't act like you never ate this shit," he said.

"Hell nah I ain't," I said laughing. I had heard of rice and pork and beans but not grits.

"Yo ass probably put sugar in yo grits," he said.

We debated about who was the most country until Jar's phone rang. Jar had already paid Eric the counterfeit two million dollars. That showed he didn't have a clue about the street life. If he was smart, he would've told us to wire the money to an overseas account. However, we did think he would notice if we put a tail on him, so instead of doing that, a couple of Jar's soldiers had been following Lisa's every move to make sure Eric did the job. We also had inside men working for us. After Jar ended the call, he informed me that Lisa had just arrived at Eric's house. This nigga was dumb enough to kill her in his house which only made our plan better.

"Where's Amoy?" Jar asked.

"With Nova. You know she's moving to Alabama?" I asked him. His eyes grew as big as a full moon, but he immediately regained his shock.

"Nah," he answered dryly.

"So, you just gon' let her leave like that?" I asked.

"Man, what da fuck you mean?" he asked.

I chuckled. "So you still denying you like her?"

He looked around as if we weren't alone in my house. "You think she likes me like that?"

I laughed hysterically. "Yea, nigga."

He sat in deep thought for a few minutes. "Man, that girl is different. I don't mean some Amoy or Cache type different. I mean she's earthy, spiritual and peaceful.

There's so much darkness inside me, I'll only taint her. I ain't the type of nigga she needs."

"Maybe she's the type of woman you need," I told him.

"You like being all weak and in love?" he asked.

I gave his question some thought. After my mom died, I had to learn to love myself again after living with my granny. The only women that held a place in my heart were the ones in Noble's family, but it always felt like a hole was in my heart. Amoy filled that hole and consumed me. Whether I wanted to love her or not didn't matter. My heart belonged to her. Being with and loving her made me the happiest I'd been in my adult life.

"Yea, I do. Your sister didn't make me weak. She made me become a better man," I said, nodding my head.

He shook his head. "Pussy whipped mothafucka. Stop fucking my sister."

I burst out laughing.

"You think he's going to do it?" Jar asked.

"I don't know. If he doesn't, we gotta kill them both and pray we can find the tapes in that big ass house. I'm sure that's where they're hiding them," I said.

Jar and I got bored waiting on Eric's call, so we started playing Madden. Hours had passed and still nothing. Jar called his men and they said Lisa was still at the house. I called our inside man to see what was going on inside the house. He informed us Eric and Lisa were fucking as we spoke. We fell asleep waiting on the call.

"Hey! Wake up!" Amoy said, nudging me.

Jar jumped up and checked his phone. "Oh shit! That nigga done called four times."

He walked out of the room to return the call.

"Where you been? It's four o'clock in the damn morning," I said staring up at her.

"I've been hanging with Nova and getting high as hell. I'm so damn horny. I wanna make some nasty, wet, sticky sex," she said, straddling my lap. My dick started to grow.

"Let's go," Jar said, walking back into the room.

"Gimme about an hour," I said as Amoy kissed on my neck.

Jar walked over and yanked her from my lap. "Stop doing that shit in front of me. That's fuckin' disgusting. I forbid you to have sex until you are married."

Amoy looked at me to see if he was serious. I shrugged my shoulders. She giggled as I held in my laugh.

"Now, let's fuckin' go," he said, walking out the room.

I stood up. "Keep that thought until I get back."

I kissed her softly on the lips and left. We didn't waste any time getting to Eric's house. Eric was standing on the front porch pacing back and forth. We got out the car and followed him inside the house.

"Where's my money?" he asked.

"Nigga, slow down. Where's the body?" I asked.

"In the fuckin' bedroom. Hurry and get it out of here," he said still pacing. He was a nervous mess.

"Show us which room. This a big ass house," Jar said.

We followed him up to the third floor. Eric didn't go inside the room. I stepped in the room first to see Lisa's brains splattered all over the sheets. She was completely naked. The nigga actually fucked her before he killed her. I instantly became angry when I looked down to see I was standing in vomit. Jar stood at the foot of the bed looking down at my feet.

"Nigga fucked her before he killed her. Then vomited," he said laughing.

"Come to my study, so I can give you these tapes. I want the rest of my money wired into an overseas account," he said, walking ahead of us. Dumb ass should've done that with the first payment. I sent a text to my inside man.

Come into his study in fifteen minutes

We stood in the middle of the study watching Eric. He removed a picture hanging on the wall that had a security system behind it. Once he put in the code, a small section of the hardwood floor opened. He reached down and pulled out a backpack. I was grateful he fell for our plan because we never would've discovered the tapes without the security code. He slung the backpack at our feet.

"I take it you are men of your word, so I will give you the information to my account," he said. He walked over and sat at his desk. Jar and I took a seat on the opposite side. The study door came open.

"Luther, what the hell are you doing in here? You are supposed to be guarding the house," Eric asked his bodyguard angrily.

"His presence is needed here," Jar said.

Luther walked over and placed his phone in my hand. I sat and watched Eric blow Lisa's brains out before passing the phone to Jar. He smiled as he watched it. Eric sat behind his desk nervous and confused. Jar passed him the phone. Eric sat with his mouth open and tears in his eyes. His body was stiff as a board.

"You had something on us, now we got something on you. Here's how things are going to work. You will keep your mouth shut about Aunt Belle and your parents' deaths. I will keep this video as security. Oh and that two million is counterfeit. Spend it at your own risk," I said.

"And one other thing, I'll be using your trucking company to bring in my shipments from time to time. I'm sure you won't mind, since you wanted to become a criminal so bad," Jar said with a smile.

"Get the hell out!" Eric demanded as he stood up. Our eyes zoomed in on the big wet spot on his pants. We burst out into laughter.

"The cleanup crew is on the way to take care of the body," I told him.

"Thanks for your services," Jar said, shaking Luther's hand. We paid Luther a half a million to place a recording device in the bedroom.

"Hey, there's a thousand damn rooms in here. How did you know which room to record?" I asked Luther.

"That's where he fucks all his women. He calls it the Boom Come Getcha Some Room," Luther said smiling. We laughed harder.

"Oh yea mothafucka, I quit," Luther said staring at Eric.

Two Weeks Later

Cache

"**S**he's so frail," I said to John as I stood on the side of my mom's hospital bed.

He closed his eyes for a brief moment. "She mostly sleeps now. She can barely talk at all. The medication doesn't do much for the pain," he said looking at her.

"Thank you for being here for her," I said, hugging him unexpectedly.

"I love her. I wouldn't be anywhere else. She told me the true reason she left you with your father," he said. I looked at him urging him to continue. "Your mother has been sick for a while and needed her parents' money to get the best medical care possible. She didn't want your father struggling with her medical bills and trying to provide the best life for you. Her parents' terms for paying for her care was that she returned home. I know it doesn't heal you of the pain of feeling rejected by your mother, but I just thought you should know," he said.

My tears flowed down my chubby face. "Why didn't she ever tell me?"

"She always thought she would get the transplant in time to mend things with you," he informed me. I cried harder and he held me until I stopped.

"I'm going to go home and get some rest. You don't have much longer," he said in reference to my enormous belly.

"Any day now," I said with a smile.

After John left, I sat there with my mom wishing she was awake so I could tell her about my honeymoon and our beautiful home. We were still living in his place until we furnished our new home. I started thinking of all the years I wasted resenting my mom. The more I thought about it, the angrier I became. I pulled out my phone to call Stephanie.

"Where are my loving grandparents?" I asked sarcastically.

"You know it's Sunday; it's their country club day," she said, laughing.

"Ok," I said, ending the call. I kissed my mother on the forehead and left her room. It was time to confront my grandparents for the last time. Only this time it wouldn't be privately like they were accustomed.

*****

I pulled in front of the country club for the valet. It was lunch time, so I made my way to the dining area. I spotted them sitting at a beautifully decorated round table. There were two other couples sitting at the table with them. I waltzed over to the table.

"Hello family," I said, rubbing my belly with a huge smile on my face.

My grandmother sat there looking at me with her mouth slightly opened. My grandfather smiled at me nervously.

"Well, seems like the cat has granny's tongue, so I'll introduce myself," I said to the table.

"Catherine." She finally spoke, glaring at me. I ignored her.

"May I?" I pulled out an empty chair at the table. The gentlemen sitting next to the chair stood to assist me. "Why thank you," I said with a smile.

"Catherine, this is not the place." My grandmother stared at me.

"Oh but, Granny, this is the best place," I replied. The other woman at the table bore a shocked expression at the revelation that her friend was my granny. The woman's face was plastered with confusion.

"Yes, she is my loving grandmother. Priscilla, her daughter, married my black father and their love created me. When I was eight years old, Granny here told my mother if she wanted to return to the family, she would have to abandon her marriage and her only child. See, they couldn't have their family being tarnished with a black grandchild. Their white blood is too pure. They used my mother's sickness to get her to turn her back on me and my father instead of helping her like loving parents should do," I said, turning to stare at my granny. I started to get sharp pains below my abdomen. I twitched in my seat trying to relieve the discomfort. Everyone remained quiet at the table.

"You are an evil, racist, low ass human-being. What gives you the right to think you are superior to me because you are white? You should learn history, Granny. Black women are the mother of this earth. But trust me; we don't want any parts of your kind. I was eight damn years old and you snatched my mother away from me to save your lily-white high-class reputation. But at the end of the day, you are still the lowest form of a human being on this earth," I said with malice. I stood up as the pains became worse. I saw Stephanie coming in our direction.

"And my spineless grandfather, get a fucking backbone and stand up for yourself. You are living in misery for the sake of a good life with her money," I said to him.

I looked around the table at everyone. They all were wide-eyed with their mouths wide opened. An unbearable pain shot through me, and I grabbed the bottom of my stomach. I looked at Stephanie letting her know I needed help, and she rushed to me.

"I'm in labor," I said in a low tone.

"Oh my God, we gotta go!" she screamed. I was unable to walk because the pains were becoming so severe.

"I need someone to help get her to the car!" She requested.

I was bent over trying to relieve the pain. Two men sitting at a nearby table jumped up to assist us. They lifted me up, one on each side of me, and placed me in Stephanie's car. She hopped in the driver's seat and rushed me to the hospital.

"Call Noble," I said with excruciating pains shooting through me.

Stephanie immediately called his phone. "Get to the hospital! I'm headed there now! Cache is in labor!" She looked over at me and placed her hand on my shoulder as she drove.

"I'm so glad I decided to come to the club after you called me. Something told me you were going there to confront them in front of their friends," she said, smiling.

"I'm sorry. I know they're your grandparents too, but I had to, Step," I said, taking breaths trying to ease the pain.

"Don't be sorry. I'm glad you finally did it. Nana's face was so red, and Papa could barely look you in the eyes," she said laughing. I laughed through the pain with her. Stephanie was running every red light and damn near killed us a couple of times.

"I'm going in to get them," she said, hopping out the car at the emergency entrance.

"Oh shit! Hurry up, Step! I think my water just broke!" I screamed as she jumped out of the car.

A few minutes later, they came rolling out a gurney. They opened the door and lifted me on the gurney and rushed me inside. Once they had me in a room, they hooked me up to machines to start monitoring me.

"Where's Noble?" I asked, looking around the room.

"Is that the baby's father?" a young white nurse asked.

"Yes," I answered starting to become emotional.

"He hasn't arrived yet, but I'm sure he's on his way," she said to calm me down.

After she was done checking all my vitals, she informed me that they were going to check to see how far I had dilated.

"The father is here. He's on his way in here," an older, white nurse said to me as she walked in the room.

A huge relief came over me. A few minutes later Noble came in the room. He leaned down, kissed my forehead, and held my hand. I could look at his face and tell he was nervous, but he tried to remain calm to keep me calm.

"I'm going to check to see how much you've dilated. Just try to relax as much as you can," the older, white nurse said before positioning her hand inside me. My face scrunched up at the discomfort she was causing.

"Just try to relax," Noble said looking at me with his soft brown eyes.

"Whew, it won't be long. You are already seven centimeters," she said, lifting her head up smiling at Noble and me.

"I need something for this pain," I said as another intense contraction took over my body.

"I'm sorry, you're too far dilated. Giving you medication right now will slow down your delivery," she said with remorse.

"I don't give a fuck! This shit hurts! I'll stay pregnant another day!" I screamed at her. She smiled and walked out the room.

"Baby, you gotta calm down. We're almost there," Noble said, squeezing my hand.

Just as I opened my mouth to cuss Noble out, another contraction took control of me. I groaned from the pain that was ripping through me.

"Here is some ice chips to keep your mouth from being so dry," the young nurse said giving the cup to Noble. I knocked Noble's hand away from my mouth as he tried to feed me the ice chips.

"Ain't shit funny, nigga. This shit hurts." I yelped angrily at him.

He leaned down and whispered in my ear. "It wasn't hurting when you was making our baby."

I continued cussing Noble out as the labor pains continued off and on for about fifteen more minutes. In between contraction he would laugh at my misery, but he showed me empathy when one hit. My doctor finally came into the room.

"Hi, we are bringing a beautiful baby girl into the world today. I'm going to check you to see if we're ready," she said, standing at the foot of my bed. My body tensed up again feeling the discomfort of her examination.

"Let's get her to the delivery room," she said to the older nurse. "I see you are already suited up and ready," she said smiling at Noble.

After about twenty minutes of screaming, pushing, and cussing everyone out, I delivered an eight pound, four ounces beautiful baby boy. The doctor placed him in my arms after cleaning him. All I could do was look at him and cry. To feel that much love for someone in only a few minutes was indescribable. I looked up at Noble, and I could see tears of joy in his eyes.

"We did it, baby," he said. He reached for him, and he cradled his son in his arms. I looked at them both with a full heart. I couldn't ask for a better person to spend the rest of my life building a family with. Of course, our healthy, handsome boy was named after his father.

Six Weeks Later

Noble

Before leaving the hospital, Cache wanted to stop by her mother's room so she could see her first grandson. Priscilla could barely open her eyes, but she forced a smile. Cache didn't want to leave her mother's bedside, but I had to get her and our son home to rest. She promised her mother she would be there every day to visit her so she could see Noble Jr., and Cache hadn't broken that promise yet. I took her and Noble Jr. to the hospital every day at noon. It was hard for Cache to deny the inevitable regarding her mother's fate, but she prayed every day that she would pull through.

I had just awaken from a nap to find Cache holding our son like always. It was a beautiful sight to see her and him together, but I didn't want her spoiling him.

"You're going to spoil him sitting there holding him like that," I said, gently taking him from her arms and placing him in the bassinet.

"I'm his mother. That's what I'm supposed to do," she said smiling at me.

"You better take a nap while he's sleeping. I gotta work the lounge tonight, so you'll have him to yourself," I reminded her.

"Dinah is bringing Stella over for a couple of hours," she said nervously.

I didn't have a problem with Stella coming over, because Dinah had been doing what she was supposed to do as a mother. We hadn't seen Stella in a couple of weeks, so we were definitely missing her. Dinah was still waiting to see how much time, if any, she would have to do. I hadn't spoken to her lawyer since we had gotten back from our honeymoon, but he had been working to get her the least amount of time as possible. Being a snitch was off the table.

I noticed Cache sitting on the chaise staring at her phone. Her hand was shaking, so I walked over and looked at the phone. It was John's phone number. I slowly took the phone from her hand as her eyes filled with tears. Just as we suspected John was calling to inform us that Priscilla had passed away. I didn't have to tell Cache what the call was about, because she felt it in her heart. I ended the call and laid down on the chaise with her in my arms. She cried softly until she fell asleep. I called Dinah to let her know

Cache couldn't babysit Stella for her today. I was surprised that she was more concerned with Cache's well-being than not having a babysitter. She was becoming the person she needed to be for Stella.

The next day Cache prepared for her mother's burial with the help of Stephanie and Amoy. She actually put her feelings aside and had decent conversations with her grandparents about the preparations for the service. Their acceptance didn't matter to her anymore. She only wanted to make peace within herself. She didn't feel the need to forgive them, but only to heal her heart from their rejection. Cache didn't see how forgiving them would help her heal if they didn't see their wrong-doings, and I totally understood her not forgiving them.

Two Days Later

My parents came down early so they could stay home with Noble Jr. while we attended the burial. All her mother's family was there. Priscilla's parents wanted her buried in the family plot, but Cache refused. We purchased lots so she could be buried with our family.

The service was beautiful. Everyone came to show support for Cache. Nova sung a song at Cache's request. After the services, the family accepted guests at the church's dining hall where food was served. I could look at Cache and see how tired she was. I promised myself as soon as she returned for her checkup, I was taking her away for a week of rest.

We were finally back home after everyone left the church. Cache was in the bedroom taking a nap, and my mom and dad were sitting there enjoying their grandbaby. I went to answer the door for Dinah when I heard the bell ring; I knew seeing Stella would make Cache happy. Dinah went into the den to visit my parents while I took Stella upstairs. I could hear Cache's soft cries on the other side of the bedroom door. I quietly opened the bedroom door to see her in a fetal position with her back to the door. I walked over and stood over the bed.

"Someone's here to visit you," I said softly.

"Baby, please give whoever it is my apologies. I'm just not up for talking right now," she said never turning to face me.

"I think you'll want to see this person. I'm sure they wanna see you," I said. She took a deep breath.

"Who is…?" she started to ask as she rolled over.

Her face lit up with a beautiful smile that I hadn't seen since our son's birth. She laughed and cried as she reached for Stella. She held Stella in her arms tightly and smothered her chubby face with kisses.

"Dinah's downstairs. I'll give you some time with Stella?" I said, walking away.

"Thank you," she said smiling at me. I leaned down and kissed her softly on the lips.

I went downstairs and seemed to have interrupted a serious conversation between Dinah and my parents. All their faces held solemn looks. My parents sat beside each other on the sofa while Dinah sat on the love seat. I walked over and sat in my recliner.

"What's going on?" I asked, glancing around the room at them.

"I spoke with the lawyer this morning. The best he can do is eight years with the possibility of parole in four. I will have to wear an ankle monitor until I'm off parole," she said sadly.

"That's fuckin' bullshit. This is your first offense," I stated angrily.

"I know and we both know why they're doing this. They want me to snitch," she said.

"It's up to you, Dinah. I can't make that decision for you. The best thing I can do is help you to move if you choose to snitch," I told her.

"I don't want to put Stella's life in jeopardy. If I snitch, they'll come after me regardless of where I'm at," she said.

"We've agreed to take care of Stella until she's released," Ma said.

Cache walked into the room with Stella in her arms. By the expression on her face, she heard the conversation. She looked at Dinah with sadness in her eyes. I knew she was going to act a fool about Dinah not wanting her to keep Stella while she did her bid, but she shocked me.

"I promise to help with her. We can keep her over the summer if that's okay with you, Dinah," she suggested.

Dinah smiled. "I would love that."

"We will make sure to bring her to visit you every weekend," Dad told her. Dinah started to softly cry. Ma walked over and consoled Dinah as she wept.

"Thank you all so much. I know I don't deserve what you are doing for me, but I truly appreciate everything from the bottom of my heart," Dinah said, wiping her tears.

Amoy

"You sure you don't mind?" Cache asked me as I sat holding Noble Jr.

"Of course not. I need some time to bond with my nephew. Yo ass been being so greedy with him," I said, rolling my eyes at her.

She laughed. "I'm sorry. I'm just so in love with him."

"Well I know you and Noble need your alone time since you've been cleared of your six-week checkup. Just don't be trying to make another one so soon," I warned her.

"Don't worry I'm not. I'm taking a year off from school, because when I start back, I'm taking a full course loads each semester. So, I'm going to use this year to enjoy my baby boy," she said.

"We ain't raising baby boys around here. I done told you to stop babying him," Noble said, walking into the den with Dachon.

Nova laughed. "He is a baby." Nova was moving away tomorrow. We had all gone out to celebrate her new job and move, but I could tell she was disappointed that Jarvis didn't show up.

"Girl, don't pay him no mind. He acts like he's a damn drill sergeant around here," Cache said waving him off.

"I gotta few drills I'm gon' show you tonight," he said smiling at her. She blushed like a schoolgirl in love.

"We'll take him to your house since you got the big king size bed," I told Dachon.

"You two might as well move in together. You're either staying at his house or he's at your house," Cache said.

By the look on Dachon's face it wasn't anything he was interested in doing with me. He quickly changed the subject and it crushed my heart. We had been spending so much time together over the past two months, so I thought he was ready to take our relationship to the next level. I had mentioned us moving in together to him, since we spent every night together, but he ignored my suggestion and changed the subject.

Our relationship had endured so much; I thought he loved me enough to want more with me. We didn't have any lies, secrets, or betrayals between us anymore. Lisa and Eric got the karma they had coming. Eric was allowing Jar and Noble to use his trucking company to push their product. Juan was now their connect, so they were making crazy money. I thought my life was finally coming together. This was why I had always been afraid of giving someone my heart. Once they had it, they didn't give a damn about it.

Noble went to answer the front door when the bell rang. He came back into the den with Jar, who didn't even look at Nova.

"Y'all having a party and didn't invite me?" he asked.

"We did invite you. We all went out and celebrated Nova's move. She's leaving tomorrow," I said.

He gave Nova a blank stare. "Good luck on that."

She walked over and stood in front of him. "That's all you gotta say to me?"

"What da fuck else I'm supposed to say? You ain't my bitch. Go find some country ass nigga and make homemade jam or something," he said, walking away from her.

"That's mean, Jar," I said.

"That's okay, Amoy. He's just a lost little boy," she said shaking her head as if she felt sorry for him. She said her goodbyes and promised to call us before she left the next day.

"So y'all took the baby to the club?" Jar asked.

He knew I was going to get in his ass for the way he treated Nova, so he tried to distract me. But I wasn't going to say anything to him about Nova; if he didn't realize how great she was, I wasn't going to try to convince him. Besides, the man that claimed to love me wouldn't even move in with me. I was in no place to tell Jar how to treat Nova when Dachon was starting to pull away from me already.

"No you, idiot. Daddy kept him for us. Amoy and Dachon are keeping him tonight for us," Cache said.

"Oh yea. Six weeks up. You bout to get fucked da hell out of tonight," Jar said nodding his head.

Noble slapped him in the back of the head. "Fool, shut up."

A Few Hours Later

"What's the stank attitude about, Amoy?" Dachon asked me lying on the bed watching television.

I ignored his question and kept searching his house for my purse. I was starting to get frustrated because I couldn't find my purse anywhere. My cellphone was in my purse and I needed to call Cache to make sure I fed Noble Jr. at the right times.

"Where da fuck is my purse?" I asked him angrily.

He ignored me the same way I ignored him. I sucked my teeth and went downstairs to search for my purse. There it was lying on the couch. I could've sworn I took it upstairs with me last night after we came from visiting Cache and Noble. I searched my purse for my cellphone but couldn't find it. I was so upset about Dachon's rejection to move together that I wasn't thinking straight. It dawned on me that I put it on the charger in his study.

I went to grab my phone that was lying on the desk to call Cache, but my eyes stretched open as I stared at the little black box lying beside my phone. I picked it up and opened it to see an enormous princess cut diamond ring with baguettes. My heart was pounding as I made my way back upstairs with the ring in my hand. Dachon was in the bathroom and Noble Jr. was asleep in the bassinet we had bought him for his sleepover. I opened the shower door to see his wet, dark chocolate body covered in suds. I just stood there holding the box waiting for him to say something.

"You don't move in with the woman you plan to spend the rest of your life with. You marry her," he said smiling.

"Oh my God! Yes, yes, yes!" I screamed, jumping in the shower fully clothed. He leaned down and sucked my tongue into this mouth. We started tearing my wet clothes from my body. I could feel my center throbbing to have him inside of me. Unfortunately Noble Jr. had other plans for us. I could hear his soft cries coming through the monitor Dachon had brought into the bathroom with him.

"He's hungry but Cache has specific times she feeds him," I said getting out the shower and wrapping a towel around me.

"Yea Noble told me about that bullshit. He said to feed his son when he starts whining for a bottle, because Cache on that white people shit with scheduling feeding times," he said, getting out and wrapping a towel around his waist.

He took the ring from my hand and slid it on my finger, and it fit perfectly.

"I love you," I said softly.

"Walking yo ass around here pouting about bullshit," he said, smacking me on the ass. I giggled.

"I was scared, because I thought you was having second thoughts," I confessed.

"Only second thoughts I'm having is on the number of babies I'm putting in you," he said smiling at me.

We went back into the bedroom, and he sat beside me on the bed as I fed Noble his bottle. I couldn't wait to give him all the beautiful chocolate babies he wanted.

Epilogue

Two Years Later

Dachon and I got married nine months after he proposed. We had the perfect honeymoon in Brazil, and we moved into a beautiful mini mansion on the same road as Cache and Noble. My wedding was everything I wanted it to be. Jar walked me down the aisle. Cache and Stephanie were my only two bridesmaids, because Nova couldn't make it to the wedding. She said she wasn't able to get off from work, but I think she didn't want to see Jar.

She would be surprised at the man Jar had become. He was a drug kingpin and a business mogul. Jar would never admit that Nova's leaving affected him, but I knew it had. She was the only one that could calm him so easily when he became furious. They built a platonic bond that was stronger than most relationships, and he just let her walk away. His entire attitude and demeanor had changed over the past two years. The only thing he cared about was making money and keeping his life organized. He cleaned everything of Aunt Belle's out of our parents' house and made it his home. Jar and Noble bought Eric's trucking company, and no one knew what happened to Eric. He just disappeared. I was sure Jar and Noble had something to do with that happening, but I didn't care. He was a waste of oxygen.

Cache and Noble were doing great. She was back in school and juggling being a mom. She was handling everything like a pro. They had been helping Noble's parents with Stella, and Cache would take her to visit Dinah sometimes. Cache still didn't have anything to do with her grandparents and it didn't seem to bother her anymore. Her tantrums were almost nonexistence. She only threw them now to get her way with Noble, because he was like putty in her hands.

Today everyone was in my hospital room. I gave birth to a six-pound, twelve-ounce healthy, handsome baby boy. I didn't have any say in the baby's name after we found out I was having a boy. He inherited his father's name, Dachon James Knight. He thought I would have a problem with our baby having part of his father's name, but I didn't, because he wasn't his father nor was he responsible for his father's actions. His only intentions were to love and protect me and our family for the rest of our lives together.

THE END

For Updates and Sneak Peeks:

NONA DAY'S ROMANCE READING GROUP

https://www.facebook.com/groups/137785320163038/

ON INSTAGRAM MSNONADAY

https://www.instagram.com/msnonaday/

SOUL PUBLICATIONS

CPSIA information can be obtained
at www.ICGtesting.com
Printed in the USA
LVHW031722280120
645065LV00005B/962

9 781706 473565